IQ'HER

CONQUERED WORLD: BOOK TEN

ELIN WYN

CLOCK
WALK
PUBLISHING

IQ'HER

General Rouhr let out a deep breath, sat back in his chair, and closed his eyes. "Estimates on how long our food supplies will last?"

"Unknown, sir. This could simply be a blight that is temporary or this could be the result of something far more sinister," I answered. "When Sylor killed the first set of vines, the area under cultivation affected increased by nearly nineteen percent. In the subsequent weeks, with all of the vines that had comprised the dome now destroyed, the area increased at an alarming rate of just over thirty-seven percent. More than a third of the plants on this continent, half of which were used for food, are either dying or dead."

"How quickly will that affect us?" Rouhr asked.

"If I were to put a timeframe to it, I would say at

current levels of consumption and loss, less than a year."

This would create a problem of nearly apocalyptic proportions before too long. During the nearly a year that we'd been a part of the population, I'd noticed that many humans knew next to nothing of proper distribution, use, and storage of their perishable goods.

Of course, I was a bit biased and perhaps a bit spoiled.

While living on the *Vengeance*, the food simulators were capable of taking the most basic of edible materials and could turn them into meals.

The simulators could take two tons of materials and feed sixty full-grown Valorni three meals a day for an entire year. The simulators aboard the *Aurora* were even more efficient.

However, there was a slight problem.

He let out a groan that sounded as though he had just been struck in the chest. "This is not something that I wanted to have to deal with," he said quietly. He never mumbled, but I wondered if he had said those words more for himself than for me. He looked up at me and rubbed his hands together. "So, what are your suggestions?"

"There are only two reasonable courses of action that we have, sir." I sighed. "For long-term stability, both will require investigating if the Puppet Master is involved or not. We need to understand the connection between those vines and the rest of the planet's ecosystem."

"Tell me." He pursed his lips.

"Rationing, or finding ways to create new and more efficient simulators."

He cocked his head to the side. "Could we build enough simulators?"

I shook my head. "Even if we used every system from the *Aurora*, as well as every computer system in all of Nyheim and Duvest, we would not be able to create enough simulators to feed the entire population. We would be forced to eliminate nearly eleven percent of the population in order to feed them."

"And that's obviously a terrible plan." Rouhr sighed and shook his head. "What we need is to follow your original suggestion of rationing." He clicked a button on his office comm unit. "Tobias?"

Nothing.

Another click, and static answered.

"This thing hasn't worked properly all week," Rouhr muttered. "What does it take for a general to have working hardware?"

"Would you like me to take a look, sir?" I offered.

"No," he waved the offer away. "I know resources are still tight. Everyone is doing the best they can, there's just too much to do. I'll wait my turn."

He stabbed the button again.

"Sir?" finally came the response.

"Bring me the records of our city-wide food stores, if you please," Rouhr ordered. "And request that Vidia joins us, if you would."

"Will do, sir," Tobias' enthusiastic voice answered. I smiled at Tobias' optimistic nature. He had taken the tragedy that came with our arrival in stride.

"With the amount of food we have available, and I'm guessing based on the reports I read last week," Rouhr started, "we're going to have to share some of our food with the small settlements, and we still might not have enough."

"No, sir, we won't. At least not in the long run. If every major city donates food to help out the smaller settlements, we will still only make it through a year," I explained.

"I know." He sighed. "But it will help the smaller settlements stay alive, and that is what we need to focus on. We need to find a way to save everyone, if possible."

"And if it's not possible, sir?"

"I'm not going to think about that for now," he answered. "Let's concentrate on right now and what we can do to fix all of this."

I nodded.

Tobias brought in the reports that Rouhr had

requested and we spent the next hour reviewing them with Vidia.

Finally, face tight with strain, Vidia looked up.

"There's really only one way to handle this, isn't there."

Rouhr wrapped his hand over hers and nodded. "Rationing. There's no choice."

Decision made, Vidia nodded sharply and rose. "I'll start telling people, and start contacting the other cities. This affects us all."

She left, Tobias in her wake, noting down the items she'd already started dictating from the list in her head.

"What about us, sir?"

He sighed. "You and the teams are going to need to be on patrol to make sure that first, the Puppet Master doesn't decide to stir up more trouble, and second, the people don't start to riot. And then we'll need to coordinate with the other settlements, arrange for distribution. You may need to set up guards for the food drops, just in case."

I nodded in understanding. It was the only reasonable way to proceed.

As soon as Vidia and Rouhr announced that we would need to start rationing, people would become upset. They would start demanding answers, and without any immediate answers to give, those upset people would then become angry.

Angry people weren't likely to listen to reason or take kindly to being asked for patience.

Rouhr reached for the desk comm. "Attention all strike teams. Effective immediately, we are instituting a mandatory food rationing system. I repeat, effective immediately, we are instituting a mandatory food rationing system. Meet immediately for details--"

Tobias rushed into the office, face white.

"Sir! The message… Your desk comm..."

Rouhr stopped. "What about it?"

The human male swallowed, then again. "It didn't broadcast to just the strike teams' channel."

Skrell.

"Where. Did. It. Go?" Rouhr asked, every word falling like a stone into the suddenly heavy silence.

"City-wide emergency broadcast," Tobias whispered. "All over Nyheim."

"Skrell," we said in unison.

"You better get out there," Rouhr commanded. "I'll contact the other teams to let them know immediately."

"Yes, sir," I said. I left his office and headed for the armory. I was going to need some protection.

STASIA

"CHUG! CHUG! CHUG!" Everyone screamed as they banged the bottoms of their glasses against the counter. Roddik was standing on top of the counter, waving both arms in the air as he enticed the crowd.

Only when he was satisfied with the noise, the window panes already rattling in their frames, did he bring his beer up to his mouth. With the expertise of a man that was used to drinking far too much, he downed his pint glass in no more than two seconds.

The bar exploded with applause and congratulatory whistles, and the bartender went as far as handing Roddik a congratulatory free pitcher of beer. That wasn't a good idea, the way I saw it, but what could I do? I was more than tired of playing the responsible-older-sister part, and it wasn't like Roddik listened to anything I said anyway.

Ventil was one of those hole-in-the-wall bars that seemed to be impermeable to whatever happened in the real world, and even a giant alien invasion hadn't been enough for the owner to close its doors. No more than a watering hole, it still was my brother's favorite place in the whole city.

"C'mon, Stasia." He laughed, climbing down from the counter and draping one arm over my shoulder. "Cheer up, will ya? The vines are gone, the sun is finally shining again...have a drink and put a smile on your face."

"I'm having a drink." I held up my own beer. "And I am smiling." At that, I forced my lips to curl up and showed Roddik what must've looked like a snarl.

With a dismissive laugh, he pulled me closer to him.

"You should really lighten up, sis."

"Yeah, well, it's hard to lighten up after working double shifts all week long," I said, but Roddik was no longer paying attention.

He, along with all the other men in the bar, had turned toward the various screens that lined the far wall of the room. The screens had been turned off just moments ago but, all of a sudden, they lit up with the city's emblem and the word STANDBY glowing under it.

"Attention, attention," a raspy deep voice boomed through the speakers mounted next to the screens. As for the image, it remained the same, the word STANDBY replaced with PUBLIC ANNOUNCEMENT. "Ladies and gentlemen of Nyheim. We've just been told that effective immediately, the city government is instituting a mandatory food rationing system. I repeat, effective immediately, they are instituting a mandatory food rationing system. Further information will be available from the coalition government in two days."

When the announcement ended, there was no more raucous laughter inside Ventil. Instead, there was just a deep silence, one that was fraught with tension. What were the city officials thinking?

The whole city was still reeling from the vine incident, and now they mandated a rationing system out of the blue?

"This is fucking bullshit," Roddik spat, slamming his glass down on the counter. The foam sloshed over the rim, splattering on the greasy metal counter and making a few of the men pull their elbows back. Roddik gritted his teeth hard, a furious expression on his face, and pointed toward the dark screens. "Who the hell do these *people* think they are? Food rationing? We were going hungry just a week ago!"

While most of the men nodded their agreement, I

merely sighed. Roddik had never really cared about pretty much anything, let alone politics or government. That changed after the Xathi invasion, and his political rants were a constant reminder of how much life had changed in Nyheim.

"Damn right, Roddik!" A burly man shouted from the other end of the bar, wiping the beer foam from his beard with the back of his hand. "We're not their alien soldiers. We're not their subjects!"

"Damn right we're not!" another voice cried.

"They didn't even care to tell us why," another protested, and it didn't take long before the bar was housing a chorus of protests and complaints against the sudden rationing system.

The dome had cut all of Nyheim's supply lines for long enough that most of the people in this bar had gotten to know hunger intimately.

Now that the vines had been driven back, most people were looking forward to trying to rebuild their lives, picking up the pieces that were left after the Xathi war.

Some people had nothing left.

They'd created new lives in shanty towns built out of scraps, worked together to make new jobs, to create new markets and trading economies.

And then some people hadn't.

Hadn't been able to bounce back, even to crawl back

into a path that was anything like what their normal lives were before the Xathi and the rest of the aliens had torn through our sky.

Maybe they were too traumatized.

Maybe there weren't enough resources in place to get them the help they needed.

I looked at Roddik and his friends through narrowed eyes. And maybe some just didn't want to.

I sighed, shaking my head. I couldn't tell what was going on in anyone else's head. I shouldn't judge.

Everything had been hard all around.

And whatever was going on with this announcement of rationing, it would put a wrench in everyone's plans.

"Tell you what," Roddik started, climbing up on the counter. This time, though, no one was chanting. The mood was somber, and I could already see that it'd become even more so in the days to come. "I've had it with these fucking assholes!" Roddik cried out at the top of his lungs, a vein throbbing on his forehead. The crowd shouted out its agreement, and I simply sunk deeper into my seat.

Why the hell was I wasting my day off like this?

I should just get up and go home but, somehow, I found myself glued to my seat as I observed Roddik. Even though people were eating up what he was saying, I could tell he had already had one drink too many. I couldn't drag him home, but if I left, I was pretty sure he'd get into trouble.

"These aliens come here, bringing war and death, and we're supposed to accept their rule?" Roddik continued, his voice reaching a feverish pitch. "Seriously, does anyone really believe our lives are better because of them? Just look at this city. Nyheim used to prosper before these creatures came here. Now half the houses lie in ruins, and the people we love are going hungry! How much more of this are we supposed to take?"

I leaned back in my seat, slowly drinking my beer as I took in the scene. Most people were nodding furiously as Roddik spoke, and some of them were looking at him with more than just admiration.

It was an unbelievable scene: Roddik had never been a leader of men, and I seriously doubted this was the right time for him to turn into one.

"But what the hell are we supposed to do?" someone a few tables behind me grumbled. "You want to fight those things, boy?"

Roddik seemed stumped for a few seconds, and I could almost see the gears turning inside his head as he thought of an answer.

"We don't need to fight," he finally said, his eyes burning with a kind of determination I wasn't used to seeing there. "I know that Nyheim's no longer our home. The aliens have become our rulers, I've accepted that. Thing is, we don't have to stay here. They might want to rule the city, but they'll never rule *us*!"

"DAMN RIGHT!" A few people cried out. These drunken dumbasses looked more than ready to march down the city's main avenue and protest against their imaginary alien invasion.

They had a point.

There was no denying that life had become exponentially harder after the aliens arrived here, but who was to say they were the direct cause of all our grief?

I'd be willing to give them the benefit of the doubt, but too bad they were doing a poor job of explaining their point of view to the masses.

As unbelievable as it was, most people still had no idea where the Xathi had come from, or why the hell Nyheim ended up encased in a vine dome.

I had no idea, and neither did anyone else.

Communication from high above had always been similar to the food rationing warning we just received: it was always a summary listing of what they wanted us to do, no real explanation given.

Sure, the government was entirely human. People like Vidia still held to their titles, but how much of their power did they really have with the aliens in town?

The way I saw it, the one really in charge now was that alien general.

Not that any of it mattered.

Humans or aliens...they all kept the populace in the dark.

"Who's with me?" Roddik asked. "We can leave Nyheim behind and start our own colony. No aliens, no war, no food rationing. Just us and the product of our own work."

That did it.

The moment Roddik was done, everyone in the room jumped to their feet and started clapping, some of them already chanting Roddik's name as if he was some goddamn hero.

I knew that when the morning came, and with it some brutal hangovers, a lot of these idiots would have already forgotten about this stupid rebellion.

But not everyone.

I worried all the same: Roddik was planting some dangerous seeds in his buddies' heads.

"What do you say, Stasia?" Roddik finally turned to me, the only person in the room that hadn't gotten up from her seat. "Are you with us, or what?"

I sighed.

Part of me just wanted to punch Roddik for putting me in the spotlight. The other half wondered about the possibilities. I wasn't that attached to Nyheim, anyway, and moving out of this place could be the fresh start a lot of us needed…

Pushing my chair back, I rose to my feet.

"I'm with you, Roddik," I said, tipping my beer toward him. He smiled at me, beaming with pride, and that almost made it all worth it.

Almost.

IQ'HER

I leaned back, attempting to stretch a terrible kink in my back, as the rest of Strike Team Two worked around me. We were in a warehouse on the east side of the city, several blocks away from our headquarters, attempting to organize and pack food crates that were intended for drop-offs in three of the nearby settlements.

Miraculously, Rouhr's accidental announcement yesterday hadn't resulted in the terrible reactions that I had anticipated.

Thus far, we had been lucky.

Not only were most of the people we had encountered much less angry than I had anticipated, they had also been much more giving than I had given them credit for. Of course, with Tobias in regular contact with several of the food pantry and restaurant owners, there were some people that already had an idea of what was happening, even if it was only the bare bones of the situation.

The restaurant owners and organizers of the food pantries were donating food, as were several of the farmers. They had made the selfless decision to donate what they could in order to help others. I was surprised by that fact.

"You getting lazy on us, Iq'her?"

I looked over at Rokul and his smug little smile. Just because the behemoth was several inches taller and many pounds heavier than me, he thought it would be okay to make fun of me because I wasn't able to carry as much as he could.

"Just stretching myself out, Rokul. Tella had too much fun with me last night," I joked. The rest of the team all groaned and jeered at my little rib at Rokul's expense.

He took it in stride, however. "Really? Hmph." He cracked his knuckles. "Tella would have broken you." He then tilted his head to the side. "Maybe that's why your back is messed up. You're too weak to handle my woman."

We cracked jokes at one another's expense for

another ten minutes or so as we continued to load the crates when one of the *Vengeance* crew turned city guard came running in. "What is it, Hewl?" Karzin asked.

From a technical point of view, Skotan biology was fascinating. Hewl was one of the few Skotan's whose scales were a different color than his own skin. His skin was paper-white, but his scales, when brought out, were a deep purple in color. According to Skotan history, a very small population of Skotan had scales of a different color, due to a genetic anomaly.

And as interesting as all of that was, it didn't make a bit of difference right now.

Hewl spent a moment catching his breath before answering. "Sir, one of the delivery trucks is being attacked by a pack of humans."

We didn't wait. Karzin quickly ordered the other factory workers to finish packing the crates as we gathered our gear. We were out of the factory and on our way in less than a minute.

Hewl led us to where he had seen the attack on the delivery truck. We were on the move, at a near sprint, for nearly two minutes before we arrived.

What we found was a pack of fifteen or so men and a few women surrounding the truck. They were rocking it back and forth and I could see that they had already broken the truck…one of the axles was sitting on the ground at an awkward angle.

A few of the men were trying to open the doors.

Upon our approach, Karzin was yelling to gather their attention. "Stop! You people need to stop."

One of the men turned towards us and yelled an obscenity at us. He tapped a couple of his friends on their shoulders and pointed in our direction. The crowd began to turn towards us, while three of them continued to concentrate their efforts on opening the truck.

They didn't look destitute or starving.

I could have understood that.

They were just angry.

"What are you people doing?" Karzin asked.

"None of your fucking business, alien," one of the men said, pronouncing the last word like it was a curse.

Yup. Angry.

"Actually, it is. You're vandalizing and destroying city equipment, trying to steal food that doesn't belong to you," Karzin countered.

"This food *does* belong to us!" the same human yelled back at us. His dark skin and dark hair seemed to almost absorb the light as his deep bass voice echoed off the buildings surrounding us. "You bastards are trying to steal our food and we want it back."

"We're not stealing food," I shot back. "We're trying

to make sure that other people, other humans," trying to emphasize that last word, "are fed. The plant life of your world is dying off and you're going to run out of food unless you start rationing. We're trying to help."

I wanted to let them know that we were all in this together, that we were *all* going to suffer badly, not just them. We were all in the same boat.

However, they didn't buy my explanation. "Shut the fuck up, you goddamn cyborg. You're lying to us. You just want to make sure that we're forced to obey you by keeping us too weak to fight back. That's why you're taking our food."

"No, we're not!" I fired back. "We don't want to control anyone. Food is running out. The plants and crops that we *all* use for food are dying off. We need to come together, ration our food, and share with one another. That's what we're trying to do here."

"We're telling you the truth," Takar said, stepping forward with his hands up to show that he meant no harm. "Walk away from the truck and we'll forget any of this even happened."

"Or what, orange-boy? You'll try to arrest us?" a different man, small in stature and with a scarred face, spat. "You can't take us all on."

Rokul snorted. Karzin shot him a sharp look as Sylor whispered for him to be quiet. Things were not going to go well, I could feel it.

I quickly made sure that my safety was still on, then holstered my blaster. We certainly did not want to make this a deadly confrontation. I reached into my rear pack and pulled out my gloves.

I had spent a bit of time with Sylor making these after we had first arrived. They included a small electrical charge that only activated when struck. After numerous tests, we had finally managed to properly insulate them so I wouldn't get electrocuted when I used them.

I had a terrible feeling in the pit of my stomach that this was about to become violent.

"Please." I held up my gloved hands. "All we're trying to do is make sure that everyone, and I mean everyone, has food to eat. That's all we're trying to do."

"Then you guys stop eating our food and get the fuck off our planet," the little one snapped at us.

I dropped my head and I sighed. This wasn't going to work. "Believe me, my friend, if we could return to our home, we would."

"I ain't no friend of yours," he growled. Then he turned to his crowd of friends and I read his lips. "Get them."

"Rekk," Rokul echoed my inner thoughts with actual sound. All of us, including Hewl, quickly prepared to defend ourselves.

We were outnumbered about three-to-one, and

what they lacked in training, they made up for with numbers and hatred. Four of them came right for me.

I stepped aside and pushed one by me, letting Hewl —who was behind me—have that one. I ducked under a wild swing, answering with a swing of my own to the abdomen. The glove sent a small charge into the man, causing him to scream and jump back, holding his torso.

One of the women jumped in next, swinging a wooden club of some sort at me. I ducked and dodged once, twice, three times before I was able to get within reach of her. Not wanting to hit her, but fearing that I had no other choice, I blocked her next swing of the club and lightly brought my elbow into contact with her forehead.

She stumbled back, looked at me oddly, then snarled as she jumped at me. She was wild in her attacks and I finally had enough, so I moved away from her. She wasn't in control of her club the next time she swung at me, and the momentum carried her forward. She tripped and fell, the club striking her in the stomach.

She dropped to the ground, moaning loudly and struggling to breathe. I checked to see if she required assistance, but was interrupted by a shout behind me.

I quickly turned, blocking a blow from my latest attacker, and swung my leg around, sweeping his feet out from under him. Karzin quickly punched him in the head and pushed me to the side.

A large body flew by me and collided with Karzin, taking both of them to the ground. However, the human's momentum was too much and Karzin flipped him over, landed on top of him, and bounced the man's skull off the pavement.

I looked around and quickly jumped in to help Sylor, who was being attacked by two people at once. I rushed over, grabbed the smaller of the two by the shoulder and spun him around. My left hand connected with an electrical pop on his jaw. He spun around and fell, his already injured jaw striking the ground hard.

Sylor kicked his in the groin, then snapped his knee up into the man's head. That had apparently been enough for the humans, as they began running away. Most of them, anyway.

Three were unconscious and two were already being bound by the brothers, Takar and Rokul.

"That was fun," Rokul smiled, a bit of blood dripping from his nose. He wiped it away and smiled again.

I shook my head. *Idiot.* This had been a disaster.

"Get these people secured," Karzin ordered the brothers. "The rest of us, let's get that truck taken care of."

I looked over at the truck. The front tires were flat,

one of the rear axles was broken, and the windows were shattered.

The back doors had been broken open and at least one crate of food had been dumped on the ground.

This was bad.

An absolute disaster.

And it was clear, things were only going to get worse.

STASIA

"Table six sent their order back," I sighed, placing the untouched dish back on the counter.

The line cook eyed it for a couple of seconds, shook his head, and hissed a curse through his gritted teeth.

"What now?" He stirred the contents of his frying pan in an irritated manner.

"They say the vegetables aren't fresh enough." I shrugged. I wasn't exactly surprised with the customer's complaint—even with the new food rationing system barely in place, it was hard for any restaurant in the city to keep their pantry stocked.

In fact, it was almost a miracle that Biher's, the small restaurant I worked for as a waiter, still had its doors open. One of the few still-functioning restaurants in

Nyheim, it owed that status to the stubbornness of the owner, Mr. Biher himself.

"I'll take care of it, Stasia," Mr. Biher said, smiling kindly as he grabbed the plate from the counter. I leaned against the wall and watched the old man zigzag between the tables, making his way toward the one from which the complaint had come.

Placing the dish back on the table, he clasped both hands in front of him apologetically and started saying something. From the distance, I couldn't hear what it was, but in the end the customers were smiling and didn't send the dish back.

"I don't know how you do it, Mr. Biher," I told him the moment he returned.

"Kindness and honesty," he said as he laid a hand on my shoulder. "Those two go a long way." He winked. "Of course, a discount also helps."

"Of course." I smiled, even though I wasn't sure how the hell he managed to keep his cool.

Most restaurants were doomed to failure. That was just a fact of life in the restaurant business, even when everything was normal.

To survive a war, a prison of vines, and then a mandatory food rationing...well, that was almost a miracle. And to do so with a smile was most definitely one.

To top it all off, Mr. Biher had even donated some of

the food he kept in storage. A group of aliens had showed up at the restaurant the day before, saying they were making the rounds and asking local businesses if they could donate some food to the general stockpiles, and Mr. Biher didn't even hesitate. He went straight to the pantry and donated whatever he thought wouldn't be needed immediately.

It was the noble thing to do, yes, but I wasn't sure if I would've done the same if I were in his shoes. I was just a simple waiter, though, and decisions like that were well above my pay grade.

"New client," Mr. Biher said, poking me with his elbow, and I immediately looked toward the door to see one of those green aliens, a Valorni, step inside the restaurant. A few of the other customers threw him annoyed glances, but nothing more than that. The building from which the aliens operated was just a few streets down from the restaurant, and some of them had become regulars.

At least for some people, familiarity went a long way towards normalizing the Valorni and the others as just another face in the street.

"Hello." I put a smile on my face as I offered him a menu. "Can I get you a table, sir?"

"I'm not here for lunch." He ignored the menu in my hands. "I'm looking for someone. A woman named Stasia. Does she work here?"

"That'd be me." I shifted my weight from one foot to the other, a nervous feeling taking over me. Why did he know my name, and what the hell did he want with me? Could this be about —

"Your brother said you'd be here when we were unable to reach you on your comm unit."

"Roddik?" I sighed. Of course, it had to be about Roddik. What else?

I didn't want to explain to the alien that I didn't have a working comm unit because Roddik had borrowed mine and spilled beer on it.

So far, I hadn't been able to afford a replacement.

It seemed the little asshole couldn't stay out of trouble for a single day. "What did he do this time?"

"If you could come with me, ma'am," the alien replied, more politely than I expected. "I was just told to come here and inform you that your brother has been detained. If you want, you can come with me to post his bail."

"Alright," I nodded, not sure if I should feel worried about Roddik or simply kick his ass when I saw him. I knew he was having a hard time, and that he was struggling with everything that had happened during the Xathi invasion, but I had no idea how to handle him. Even though I had gone through the same things he had, I couldn't help but feel as if I was responsible for my brother's failures.

I returned to the kitchen. "Mr. Biher," I bit my lip, worried. "I'm really sorry, but I have to leave."

"Is everything okay, Stasia?" He looked over my shoulder and toward the entrance, right where the green Valorni waited for me.

"It's about my brother," I admitted. I didn't really like to talk about Roddik's problems, but I trusted Biher. With an understanding smile, he just waved me away and I handed him the menu I was holding. I felt guilty about the fact that he'd have to work harder with me being gone, but it couldn't be helped.

"I'm ready," I told the Valorni. I tied my hair back with a small leather cord, momentarily wondering about why I even cared about my appearance. I hadn't even bothered to take off my waiter's smock.

I followed after the alien for just a few minutes, and felt even more nervous than before as a couple of guards waved us inside his building.

I had never been inside the place, and I didn't like the fact that I was now coming here to bail out my brother. There were armed guards at every corner, a lot of them aliens, and everywhere I looked, people were moving through the building at a fast pace, talking to each other in clipped sentences, the air itself vibrating with barely repressed action.

While I'd never been inside the governmental

complex before the war, it wasn't always this busy, was it?

"The detention wing," the Valorni said as we finally stepped out one of the elevators.

I eyed the large room in front of me, which must have been the administrative part of the detention wing, and felt my heart drop as my gaze finally landed on the cells on the other end of the room. Even from where I was standing, I could already see Roddik.

He sat slumped on the corner, head tucked between his knees, and he wasn't moving. In the adjacent cells were five other men I recognized almost immediately: not hard to do, since they all were Roddik's drinking buddies.

"Your brother," the Valorni merely waved toward the cell, and then left to start sorting a pile of tablets at a desk.

Heading straight toward Roddik's cell, I rapped my knuckles furiously against the plex.

"Stasia?" he mumbled, slowly raising his head. He was slurring his speech, and his eyes were bloodshot. Not only that, but his hair was a mess and he looked as if he hadn't slept at all. To say he looked like shit would be more than a fair assessment. "What are you doing here?"

"I should be the one asking you that. They said you asked for me," I threw right back at him, folding my arms over my chest. Tapping my foot against the floor nervously, I glared at him. "Well?"

"Calm down, Stasia," he smiled, pushing himself to his feet. "Everything's fine now. Thish wash just a mishtake."

"This doesn't look like a mistake," I said. I didn't even need to smell the alcohol on him. I could damn near see it seeping out of his pores as he walked towards me. I took a breath. Maybe I was being too hard on him, making assumptions that didn't fit the facts.

"Are you drunk, Roddik?"

"Me?" he said, raising both hands up in the air in an innocent gesture. "Never!" At that, his buddies burst out laughing, almost as if Roddik had said something incredibly witty and smart.

Idiots, all of them.

I wasn't going to get the truth out of Roddik, apparently. Or out of any of his buddies, for that matter. Turning my back to Roddik, I gritted my teeth and scanned the office space adjacent to the holding cells.

There were several aliens working quietly at their desks, but my eyes were immediately drawn to the group of five huddled together in one of the corners. They were wearing tactical gear and looked as if they had just gotten out of a fight. Muttering among themselves, I could guess they were filling out some paperwork while not looking happy at all.

"Alright," I said, making my way toward them and raising my voice. "Spit it out. Why the hell is my brother in a jail cell?"

IQ'HER

W ith a heavy sigh, I set down the tablet with my finished reports.

"Hello?" she called out again. "Can someone help me?"

I looked her up and down as I walked over. She was fairly tall for a human female. I could swear she was around six feet in height. I hadn't remembered seeing anyone else close to that height outside of the Urai women. Her pale white skin was covered in light freckles, something that I found to actually be appealing. Her gray-blue eyes, combined with her vibrantly rich red hair that she had tied behind her head stood out. The brothers, if they had bothered to look up, would have been jealous of her hair color, their own red-orange hair still standing in spiked mohawks.

She was… interesting.

Attractive.

Alluring.

And that wasn't want I needed to be thinking about right now

"Hello, ma'am. How can I help you?"

"Oh, so you're deaf, too," she snapped, her hands on her hips, sarcasm dripping like blood. "I've been asking for someone to explain what the hell is going on for quite a few minutes now."

"That you have," I agreed. "I apologize for not being able to meet you immediately. Our team is in the process of recording our reports, and the longer it takes for our reports to be written, the more likely mistakes will be made because we'll start to remember things improperly or simply forget things altogether."

"Let me guess." She cocked her head to the side. "You're going to 'forget' some of the stuff that happened and blame it on me, right?"

"No, ma'am," I said. "You see, I've already completed my report. I write faster than my compatriots."

"Good for you." Scorn dripped from her words. Either she wasn't happy with me or she just sounded like that naturally.

"Thank you." Hoping her mood was only a response to the situation, I responded to the words, not the tone. "Now, how can I help you?"

"Why is my brother in a box?" she pointed to the closest of the plex holding cells.

The man inside was her brother?

This was the Stasia he'd been bellowing for to come and fix things?

I took a closer look and, after a moment to get past his drunkenness, his glaring, and radiating hatred, I could see the familial similarities.

Whoever the parents of these two were, they were most assuredly prouder of their daughter.

"Your brother was part of a group of almost twenty that were attacking a delivery truck. They damaged the truck and tried to steal the food that was in the truck that was meant for a nearby settlement," I explained. As I spoke, she looked over at her brother in mortification.

"He did that?" she asked. I knew she wasn't asking because she thought I was wrong, she was asking just to get clarification of something she was dreading was true.

"Yes, ma'am."

"How 'involved' was he?"

"At the moment, I cannot divulge that information. It is something that needs to be dealt with if there is a trial."

She stood there, standing sideways, her right shoulder pointed at me as she stared at her brother. I heard the disappointment in her voice, so I could imagine the disappointment on her face as she looked at him.

"I do apologize for..." I started.

Her brother interrupted me. "You better fuckin' apologize, you bashtard," he yelled out drunkenly. "You and your kind are shtealing food from us humans-es." He slammed his fist against his cell wall. "I w-w-was just taking it back!"

"You idiot!" the woman yelled at him. "Why did you have to attack and damage the truck? You didn't have to get violent with anyone. What if it had been human guards that had checked on the truck? Would you have attacked them?"

"Yep," was his response. I could see that she hadn't expected that answer. Her shoulders dropped momentarily, then I could see her arm start to shake a little as she clenched her hand into a fist.

She shook her head, stepped up to his cell, and said something to him that I didn't quite make out.

"Shut up and get me the fuck out of here, dammit. We're family," he growled at her. Then he looked at me. "You hear that, you fuckin' black and green alien shit? We're family! Bet you don't know what the hell that is."

I shook my head as I rolled my eyes. I turned my attention to the woman as she turned her back on her brother and walked over to me.

"How much is his bail?"

I shrugged and turned to Karzin. He had heard the question, flashed me a number in sign and I shook my head as I turned back to her. I sincerely doubted that she would be able to afford her brother's bail. She didn't look like one that had an abundance of funds at her disposal.

She cut a striking figure, her height combined with a nice set of curves, long, strong legs, but all hidden by her plain clothing. No jewelry, no ornamentation or frills.

"Bail was set at thirty-five hundred credits."

She nearly blew out my eardrums as she shrieked, "Thirty-five hundred?" She turned back to her brother. "What in the holy hell did you do?"

He shrugged, obviously not concerned with the results of his actions.

She turned back to me. "I can pay most of that, but not the entire amount." While her words made the statement, her tone told me so much more. Whatever amount she was able to pay would wipe her out, and that was something she seemed to be a bit hesitant to do.

She must really have loved her brother to be able to put up with his skrell, and at that price.

"Well," her brother started in, anger burning away the last of his drunkenness, "you'd be able to afford the whole thing if you wasn't buying shit you don't need."

"You mean like our rent?" She narrowed her eyes at him. "You can't even hold down a damn job for longer than a few weeks."

"And whose fault is that?" He sighed, then pointed at me. "It's those bastards'. If they hadn't come here with their damn bugs, mom and dad would still be alive. I wouldn't have to be dealing with their death and how bad it makes me feel." His tone changed from pure anger to wheedling as he looked at her. "Please, Stasia. I can't stay here. You know I can't handle tight spaces. I haven't been able to think straight since mom and dad died. Come on, sis. Please."

He actually looked sad and a bit remorseful.

Young. Weak.

He was good. I hoped that his sister, Stasia, wouldn't fall for it.

She did.

"I can't afford the entire amount, but can you please let me pay you what I have? I promise he won't do anything stupid. Again," she added, hesitantly.

I took a deep breath, looked back to Karzin for advice, who only shrugged, and then considered Stasia.

"What's your full name?" I asked quietly.

"Don't tell him!" her brother yelled.

Ignoring her brother, she told me. "My name is Stasia, Stasia Cole. Roddik is my younger brother. He's… he's trying."

I nodded in acknowledgement. "Well, Stasia. It seems clear that you're doing more than trying. If you can promise that your brother will behave *and* show up for his hearing, I'll lower his bail by half. I don't want you having to destroy your savings for this."

Her eyes widened, and she looked to be on the verge of tears. "Thank you," she whispered, her voice rough.

I nodded. "You don't need to thank me. Just make sure your brother stays out of trouble." I ducked down a little bit, not far, to make sure she could look into my eyes. "You don't deserve having to put up with this more than once."

The look she gave me was one of grateful confusion. It was like she couldn't figure me out. I couldn't blame her.

This wasn't like me at all.

Why I had chosen to lower the bail confused even me, but something about her suggested that she already had to deal with a lot of insanity.

My lowering her brother's bail was at least something to help calm that.

What I wanted to do was keep her brother locked away, both for the safety of the city and to give her some peace.

Take her somewhere she could rest, to sleep until the tired, worried lines faded from around those striking eyes.

But I knew without asking she wouldn't want that.

Even if it really would be the best thing for her.

Stasia paid the bail, and Roddik flashed me a smug smile as he strode out of the cell. "Your alien bullshit can't hold me, fucker." He looked like was going to spit at me, but she punched him in the shoulder before he could.

"Don't do anything stupid, remember? I can't bail you out again," she snarled.

He looked at me, gave me what the humans considered a vulgar gesture with his middle finger, and sauntered out without so much as a 'thank you' to his sister.

When they were gone, Rokul looked at me, a quizzical look on his face. "Well, isn't he a wonderful slice of Kinelyan pie?"

I merely nodded.

It was hard to say anything when my thoughts were filled with images of his sister and her fiery spirit.

"Man, I'm exhausted." Roddik threw himself on top of our sofa. The whole thing creaked under his weight and, for a moment, I thought the sofa would come crashing down.

Roddik didn't seem to notice at all, kicking off his shoes lazily, leaving them abandoned on the floor, and then leaning back. Propping his feet up on top of our dingy coffee table, he then ran one hand through his hair and yawned.

"Of course, you're exhausted," I said. "You and that band of idiots were *really* busy today, huh? Breaking the law and getting into fights must have really tired you out." I shook my head for a moment, barely believing I had to spell it out like this. "What the hell were you thinking, Roddik? Did you think it was a good idea to attack that truck, huh?"

"Someone has to do something," he replied bitterly, now sitting up straight. "Aren't you tired of living like this?" he continued, gesturing toward the mess that was our cramped living room. His personal belongings were strewn across the room, almost as if he had emptied his suitcase over the floor, and a dozen dirty plates were stacked on the coffee table.

Yeah, the apartment I was renting wasn't a palace, but that wasn't exactly my fault.

There was only one bedroom, mine, and I made it a point to keep everything there tidy and organized. Roddik had the sofa in the living room, but he was so damn messy that the whole place was in complete disarray all the freaking time.

"Are you kidding me?" I frowned. "We're living like this because you're the most disorganized person I've ever met." With that, I started picking up his clothes from the floor, a laundry bag in my hand. There were a few empty bottles lying in one of the corners, and those just made me angrier. "Can't you at least clean up after yourself? I'm not your freaking mom, Roddik."

"I know you're not her," he whispered, his voice boiling with anger. That immediately made me regret my words. I had every right to be pissed at him, but to drag our parents into it…? No, that wasn't like me.

"I'm sorry. I didn't mean to—"

"But you did," he cut me short, jumping to his feet and heading toward the kitchen. I heard the food storage unit door opening, but then he slammed it shut a fraction of a second later. He was probably looking for beer, but I had emptied the fridge the night before. Roddik's drinking was getting out of hand, and I wasn't about to watch my brother drink himself to death.

"Listen, Roddik," I continued as he returned to the room, doing my best to sound amiable. It was time to practice the honesty-slash-kindness combo Mr. Biher liked to preach. "Things can't go on like this. I miss mom and dad just as much as you do...but we have to start working together. I need you to make an effort."

"Yeah, why don't you get off your high horse, Stasia?" he immediately shot back at me. "Maybe you're the one who should be making an effort."

"Me?" I laughed. By then, my amicable tone had already vanished. Screw kindness: I was more than ready to whoop his ass. "You must be freaking kidding me."

"I'm not," he hissed. "You talk about working together...so why didn't you stand up for us? Or, better, why weren't you there with us?"

"Now there's a question I can answer," I smiled sarcastically. "I wasn't there with you and your stupid friends because I have a job. One which, by the way, is paying for this apartment. Or have you forgotten about that?"

"How could I?" He rolled his eyes. "You keep throwing that in my face whenever you have the chance. I don't get you, sis, I really don't. The whole city is on the verge of starvation, the aliens are bossing us around, and the only thing you seem to care about is your stupid little job. Can't you see there's more at stake right now?"

"That's rich. You can't even hold down a job, and now you want to make things right with the world?" This time, it was my turn to roll my eyes at him. And, oh, they rolled so damn much I was actually surprised they didn't pop out of their sockets. "Why don't you start with making things right in this living room, huh?"

"God, Stasia. Are you even listening? We have to focus right now." He closed the distance between the two of us and laid one hand on my shoulder. "Okay, you're right. We need to start working as a team. Now listen...I know you still have some savings, and that's a start, but we need to figure out a way to get more money. We're gonna need it to bail out the rest of the guys. Do you think Biher would loan you some money if you asked?"

That did it for me.

His words were the last straw.

"Are you out of your freaking mind?!" I cried out. "I'm killing myself here, working night and day so that I can keep a roof over our heads. Now you want us to go into debt so we can bail your friends out? I'm lucky I even managed to get you out! If it weren't for that guy back at the station, you'd be rotting in there right now."

"*That guy*," he snorted, repeating my words in a deprecating tone. "You mean that alien? Are you siding with them over your own family now, is that what this is?"

"Are you even listening to yourself?" I tried to protest, but it was a fool's errand. There was no arguing with Roddik whenever he was like this. "I'm not friends with them but, unlike you, I can admit whenever someone's being kind to me. If you didn't have your head stuck so far up your ass, maybe you'd see that."

It was the oddest thing...Thinking about the alien made my heart flutter a bit. He was so tall, with a body that was built like it was made for combat. His eyes had a calculated, controlled alertness to them that made my skin tingle with the awareness of danger.

But when he spoke, he'd been nothing but compassionate. Kind. Understanding.

A woman could feel safe in those arms.

Roddik looked as if he was about to shout

something as a reply, but I didn't give him the time. I just turned around on my heels, grabbed my keys from the table, and bolted out of the apartment. I slammed the door behind me, probably more harshly than I had intended, and sucked in a deep breath.

"You're driving me crazy, you idiot," I whispered under my breath, completely at a loss on what to do. Roddik used to be this sweet little kid, but after our parents had died during the Xathi invasion...he simply wasn't the same.

He couldn't hold down a job, did nothing but drink the day away with his buddies, and now he had started acting out in a scary way.

What the hell was going through his head? I never thought he'd be as dumb as to go out and destroy a food delivery truck.

That wasn't the Roddik I knew.

Breathing in and out slowly, I tried to calm myself. Hopefully, this would be just a phase and things would get better soon enough. Roddik would see the light and start acting responsibly.

I *had* to believe that.

Climbing down the stairs of our apartment building, I fastened my jacket over my waiter's uniform. No one was expecting me back at Biher's today, not after I had left with that Valorni, but after paying for Roddik's bail, I could use the extra shift.

There was nothing quite like work to keep my mind occupied.

From thoughts of my brother's idiocy.

And the strong arms of the alien with the kind eyes.

IQ'HER

At the removal of Roddik the drunken idiot, things should have gotten quieter without him there to instigate stupidity. That was nowhere near the case.

"Hey, ugly-ass alien guy! Why are you trying to take food away from us humans?"

I wasn't sure which one had asked the question, and since the rest of the team was gone doing our actual duties, I was left to deal with these fools. I turned towards the cells and wondered for the fortieth time since we arrested these men, why we had decided to rebuild the *Vengeance* brig here in Nyheim.

Back on the ship, the detention cells were clear, so the offender would be embarrassed by their actions.

It worked, too.

We rarely ever used the brig. No one wanted to be the one locked up for everyone to see.

But these four idiots counted their time in the cells as a badge of honor, like it was something worth bragging about to the rest of their troop of malingerers.

Then, the one in cell three, a skinny one with a bad mustache, wearing shorts, and with vulgar tattoos covering both legs — although, the tattoo artist was talented... I never knew how a hairy, naked human woman would look until I saw his left calf — spoke up. "I'm talking to you, you alien bastard."

"Really?" I snapped back. "I hadn't noticed. I thought you were trying to hold a conversation with that ugly beast just under your right knee."

He looked down at this leg, then snapped his head up at me, trying to bore a hole in my head with his eyes. "That's my grandmother, you shit."

I held my tongue on my next comment. Whoever had butchered that poor woman's looks deserved to be shot...unless she truly did look that bad, then...I cleared the thought from my mind. "What makes you think we're trying to steal your food?"

"You and your *boss* called for us to start rationing our food, then you're taking it away from us and boxing it all up," he said, spittle from his mouth splattering the clear wall of the cell. I took a closer look at him as he spoke.

His teeth were yellowed and crooked, his mustache was ill-trimmed, and his neck was ringed with dirt. He kept scratching himself there with fingers that were also yellowed and had blackened, cracked nails. I also noticed the ring on his left third finger, an indication amongst humans that he was married.

I repressed my instinctual gag reflex at the idea that anyone was willing to attempt to procreate with this man. Either she had been forced into it, or…I didn't complete the thought. Thinking about him possibly having sex with anyone made my stomach turn at least three times.

I took a deep breath to quell my turning stomach, and to answer his question. "We called for a rationing system because the food that *all* of us eat, including those of us that aren't human, is running out. The plants that we all use are dying. As for the food that is being collected, we're doing that so we can help out the smaller settlements and keep them all alive."

"Bullshit," spat one of the others, the one that I had originally thrown past me to Hewl when the fight had started. He sported a very impressive black eye and bruise across the entire left side of his face. Hewl had not gone gentle on that one. "You're a fucking liar."

"Yeah," Mustache said. "If you hadn't arrived and brought your damn bugs with you, we would be living just fine."

I dropped my head in frustration. "For the last time, we didn't come here on purpose, and those weren't *our* bugs. The Xathi are a scourge across the entire universe and we're fighting against them. Did you not see us trying to kill them all?"

"Yeah, after you brought them here," Bruise spat. The other two joined them in their ridicule and berating of me and the others.

It wasn't going to matter what I said to them, they already had their feelings about us. I had held out hope that the 'anti-alien' groups would have tempered their feelings about us after the Xathi were eliminated and they saw that we were doing our best to repair the damage we had inadvertently caused.

I was wrong. There were still groups out there that hated us, and apparently there was one in Nyheim that was willing to get violent with their opinions. I stuck it out, doing my best to ignore their jibes, verbal jabs, and insults, for nearly an hour before the next shift started.

"Oh, thank the cosmos," I said to myself when they walked in and were human guards. "These four are under arrest for attacking a food truck, and then us. Be careful, though, they don't know how to shut up."

"Oh, look. Alien-loving shit-bags!" I heard Mustache call out. The three guards went a little red in the face at the insult.

"Kind of them to demonstrate their best qualities." I

shook my head. "They love to talk. Not very original in their insults, but they're stubborn and nonstop."

"Alien fucker!"

"As stated," I waved dejectedly.

"What do you want us to do, sir?" the lead guard asked.

"Do your best to ignore them, make sure they at least have something to drink, and…" I shrugged and raised my voice to be sure the prisoners could hear me. "If necessary, fill their cells with excrement."

Their eyes went wide. "Really?"

I looked back at the prisoners, thoroughly enjoying their glares and semi-pleading looks. "Eh. Use your best judgment," I answered. I left the building quickly, and headed to one of the restaurants Sylor had recommended to me. Not his ramen place, I wasn't fond of the noodles they used, but to another place where they served something called barbeque. Food was in short supply, but this restaurant, like many others, was skilled at stretching their reserves in ever-creative ways.

I could smell the aroma of grilled meat from far away. If it was anything like my grandmother's outdoor cooking, I felt that I would enjoy the place. As I made my way there, I saw a small group of humans, maybe seven in number, walking towards me on the street.

I was a little nervous. While I knew I was a better

fighter than them, seven-against-one odds was not something I wanted. Instead of being incompetent, unintelligent kouters like the ones we had arrested, these humans were polite. They greeted me with a smile, one of them shook my hand, thanking me for my part in taking the vines down, and then went about their business.

I felt a little silly at thinking they might attack me, or at least treat me badly. Not all humans were moronic idiots like the ones in the cells. My hope was that their whole number was what we had fought a few streets over. If the faction was that small, we could handle them.

Then again, it only takes a tiny spark to burn an entire countryside.

I arrived at the restaurant and was directed to a small private booth in the corner. I was able to see the entire common room, and there was an emergency exit only a few feet away from me. It was like I had reserved this particular seat.

It was a decently busy night, nearly two-thirds of the tables were currently occupied. A few members of the *Vengeance* ground crews were inside, sitting on the far side, otherwise it was primarily a human presence.

But there was only one human in particular that caught my eye. Vibrant red hair stretching down to the middle of her back, fantastic hips that led to legs that seemed to go on forever, and amazing, lightly freckled skin.

And loyal and filled with an indomitable spirit.

She was glorious.

Somehow seeing her the second time struck me harder. Made me want… things, things I couldn't quite explain, even more.

"Stasia?" I called out gently.

She turned at the sound of her name, recognized me…sort of hard to miss the only one here with shiny black skin covered in green circuitry that helped me move faster. She held up a finger to tell me to wait, finished what she was doing at the table she was at, then came over.

"Hi." Her eyes locked on mine and our gazes held for more than a few seconds. "I wanted to thank you for what you did earlier. I didn't even catch your name."

"I'm Iq'her, from *Vengeance* Strike Team Two." I shrugged. "It was no trouble. You looked like you needed the help, so I helped."

"Well, thank you. I mean it," she said sweetly, and I saw her cheeks start to redden as my eyes kept drinking hers in. "What can I get for you?"

"Well, what's good?" I asked. A warmth spread through me at her soft voice. She was a different type of human than those others, for sure.

"I suggest the ribs, with a side of rice." She flushed. "The salad isn't as fresh as it could be, right now."

"Thank you, yes, then that's what I'll have." I offered an answering smile.

Watching her walk away, I worried.

Not about her working here. The restaurant was clearly a nice place to work; she seemed at ease with her co-workers, the friendly calls from regular patrons.

But that brother of hers.

She wasn't anything like him. Well, maybe the temper was similar, but she at least seemed to have a brain in her skull that was used for more than simple things.

She looked out for him, whether he deserved it or not.

But did she have another looking after her?

Probably not. If she had a mate, a partner, even a best friend, she wouldn't have looked so all alone in the detention wing.

If I was her mate, she'd never have had to deal with something like that alone.

Of course, I wasn't.

That was ridiculous.

But still, her brother was obviously one of the anti-alien faction. And hot-headed, and prone to violence.

And from what I could see, his associates were no better.

Stasia's safety was in danger with every moment she spent with them.

No. I needed to find a way to protect her. I needed to be able to ensure that she was safe - especially if she stayed in the presence of her reckless brother and his hate-filled compatriots.

What if they planned something even more dangerous?

What if they somehow involved her?

I could...

My fingers tapped against one thin plate of the wrist guard of my other arm.

Before the Xathi war, I'd been assigned to infiltrate crime rings on my homeworld. The modifications to my suit had been minor, but useful. One of the additions I'd deployed was a series of tiny transmitters to record conversations and send them back to my base equipment.

And I still had one in my suit.

If I slipped one onto Stasia, I could find out if her brother was planning anything else. Anything that would put her at risk.

It was a terrible idea.

She'd hate it, if she found out.

It was an invasion of her privacy.

But if it kept her safe, it was worth doing, wasn't it?

When Stasia came back, I already had a transmitter

raised to the surface of the wrist-guard, easily flipped out with a flick of the wrist. It was ridiculously small and did a fantastic job of sticking to skin.

With its flat surface, she wouldn't notice it...I hoped.

"I want to apologize about my brother's behavior." She set down my drink. "I don't know what's wrong with him, but he didn't used to act that bad."

"It's okay," I said. "People say stupid things when they're stressed. I have a friend whose mouth doesn't always keep up with his brain, so he says the dumbest things at times. We still forgive him."

She chuckled a bit at that. I stood up and gently patted her shoulder, quickly placing the transmitter on her neck as I moved a stray hair away. I shivered in pleasure as my hand touched her smooth, delicate skin. Her bare skin was a shock to my system.

I wanted to caress her. To feel more of her.

And instead, I was betraying her trust, even if it was for her own protection.

I brought my emotions in check and tried to act professional. "You are a strong woman with a hard responsibility. You deserve to be treated better than that."

"Thank you." She paused for a moment, and rested her fingers where I'd touched her. It didn't upset the transmitter, and I got the feeling that she did so because I touched her, not because she was suspicious.

She left to deal with other customers, but I saw the small corners of her lips turn up in a smile when she left.

That made me smile, too.

When my food arrived, I ate it with zeal. It wasn't my grandmother's cooking, and there wasn't much, but it was *good*.

I left a large tip for Stasia and left.

Now I just had to be patient about the transmitter, and smother the sneaking feelings of guilt that were starting to disturb me.

It was for her protection. It had to be done.

"Thank you for coming back for the rest of the night, Stasia." Mr. Biher pushed a bundle of credits into my hands. "When Kent didn't show up for the dinner rush, I was a little worried." He folded my fingers over the credits. "It's not much, but—"

"Thank you," I cut him short, pulling him in for a quick hug. I knew the restaurant's finances were always tight, so his gesture meant the world to me. Sure, he had just given me a few credits on top of my regular pay, but that would definitely help the moment rent was due.

These days, every credit counted.

We closed up together and, when I offered to walk him home, he declined with a gentle smile. "No need," he said. "I might be an old guy, but the city is still a safe place." I wasn't so sure about that, but let him go on his way all the same. It was only a short walk from the restaurant to his apartment, so I doubted anything would happen in the way.

Besides, I had a place I needed to be.

Walking through the deserted streets, the sky above littered with as many stars as there were grains of sand, I made my way toward Ventil. No more than a few streets away and I started hearing the usual chatter of a crowded bar, the sound of deep laughs and cups banging against the tables drifting out onto the street.

I wasn't exactly in the mood for a night out, but Roddik had sent one of his friends by the restaurant with a message, asking me to meet him after work. I thought of ditching him, but the idiot would probably just get in trouble again. If I were there, at least I'd be able to keep an eye on him. Not that it mattered much — these days it was almost impossible to control him.

"And there she is," Roddik announced the moment I stepped inside the bar. He jumped up to his feet and started clapping his hands together, a mocking smile on his lips. "Come to meet the common folk, m'lady?"

"Really funny, Roddik." I frowned, taking a seat at his table. Only men were there, most of them factory workers from the industrial precinct, but they all scooted to the side so that I could fit in. They weren't bad guys, for the most part, but it saddened me that the current situation was making them bitter.

My thoughts turned to Iq'her. How nice he'd been. Somehow, with him I felt safe. When he had touched my neck, I had to keep myself from shuddering, from the crazy sensation that my knees were about to give way.

But that was ridiculous. The last thing I needed to do was throw myself at the big, sexy alien.

That would cause far more complications than I could handle right now. Besides, what if he already had someone waiting for him?

"Too bad Alek and the guys couldn't make it tonight, huh?" Roddik put a hand on my shoulder and squeezed hard. He was, of course, talking about the four assholes that were in a jail cell right now. The way I saw it, I was glad the little shits were still locked away.

"Maybe they shouldn't have gotten arrested in the first place." I shrugged, keeping my face neutral as I accepted the beer one of the guys handed me.

"Or maybe you shouldn't have left them there to rot," Roddik replied, his words turning sour.

What the hell was his problem? Had he invited me here just so he could piss me off even more?

"C'mon, Roddik," one of the guys spoke up, grabbing my brother and forcing him to sit down. "Leave her alone, will ya? Stasia would never do such a thing, would she? She's your sister, man."

A few others grumbled their agreement, and I breathed out with relief. At least they weren't siding with Roddik and throwing me under the bus. There was still hope for them, it seemed. They weren't exactly the best people in the world, but they were the closest thing I had to family now.

The conversation quickly drifted into trivial matters, and I was relieved. I wasn't in the mood for more rants or speeches, and it felt good to relax. Roddik wasn't drinking like a maniac, so that helped, too.

Looking after him was exhausting, so I definitely appreciated the fact I could let my guard down, even if just for a couple of hours.

For a moment, I almost felt normal again.

It didn't last.

Just an hour after I arrived, two massive Valorni strolled into the bar.

It wasn't the setup for a joke, but the uneasy mood my brother had put me in made me feel like I was the punchline.

They were burly guys, their size intimidating, but they didn't seem to want to cause any trouble. They greeted everyone before walking toward the counter, ordered two beers, and then started talking with the bartender. Five minutes later, and they were leaving with a small crate.

Roddik clenched his jaw as he saw it, and I laid my hand on his arm by instinct. I didn't want him to get into trouble again, especially when he still had to show up to a hearing. The last thing I wanted was for him to be thrown back into a jail cell.

Sure, he probably needed to be taught a lesson, but I simply couldn't abandon him. My mother had always trusted me to look after him, and that was exactly what I intended to do.

"What the hell was that about?" Roddik asked the bartender right after the Valorni left. The man just shrugged apologetically, showing us his hands as if saying 'what can you do?'

"They were asking for donations," he finally replied. "I reckon the city is going short on food already."

"And you just gave it to them?" Roddik asked, his eyes wide with surprise. "What were you thinking?"

"Hey, man, I don't call the shots here. The owner told me to be accommodating if those guys came knocking, and that's what I did. It's not like they took much, anyway."

That answer wasn't enough for Roddik, I could tell. There was a glint in his eyes, the kind that only appeared when his blood started boiling. "Seriously, people? Are we just going to let them come and take our food? Who's to say they're not saving all that food for themselves? I never saw one of those big bastards go hungry, that's for sure." He stood up then, almost as if daring anyone in the bar to prove him wrong.

I almost said that they couldn't 'take' what had been freely given, but I just shut up. I didn't want to cause an argument in front of everyone.

"I think it's time we start thinking of leaving the city," Roddik continued, repeating what he had said a few nights before. This time, though, there was no applause or cheering. Everyone just seemed to contemplate what he was saying with a solemn expression, almost as if they were seriously thinking of starting a new colony by themselves.

Roddik seized the chance to continue talking, his sales pitch so perfect I was almost sure he had been practicing it. It didn't take long before most people were quietly mouthing their agreement, and that was when I decided to call it a night.

Without drawing any attention to myself, I paid my tab and grabbed my jacket.

I was already crossing the street outside the bar when I heard the door swing open. "Stasia!" I heard Roddik call after me, and I sighed as I turned around to face him. "Where are you going?"

"Home," I shrugged. "You're getting everyone riled up, and I'm tired. I'm not in the mood for rants, rebellion, or whatever it is you're up to nowadays. I just want to get into bed and forget that I exist." I started walking again, not even waiting for his reply, when I started hearing his hurried footsteps echoing through the street.

"Stasia, wait!" he insisted, grabbing my arm when he caught up to me. "Look, I know I've been acting like an asshole," he said, taking me by surprise. "And I know I haven't been there for you. It's just...it's been hard, Stasia, and I don't know how to deal with things. I miss mom, and I miss dad. Without them around, I simply can't stand the city anymore."

"And do you really think leaving this place would solve all our problems?" I asked him, not even knowing what kind of reply I wanted to hear.

"Everyone wants to give it a shot," he replied, a smile on his lips that reminded me of the kid he used to be. "Besides, it's not like we have anything to lose. War, aliens, hunger...let's just leave all that behind, Stasia. Let's have a fresh start."

"A fresh start..." I repeated, enjoying the way these three words sounded. Maybe Roddik was right. Maybe a fresh start was exactly what we needed. And who knew? Maybe once we got away from the aliens, Roddik would become the brother I used to have.

"Yes," he nodded. "I'm going to do it, sis. I'm going to leave this place behind. But I want you to be a part of it...I want you to be there with me, every step of the way. I want us to stay a family."

"So, we're going out in the woods?" I asked.

Roddik nodded.

"Is the forest safe, Roddik?"

"What do you mean?"

"I mean, I don't want to go out with you and watch you create this 'alien-free utopia' only to have us all eaten by a Kodanos or strangled to death by a tree!"

"Please," he guffawed. "The forest has gotten a lot safer since those alien bugs were driven off. We'll be fine. The wildlife is probably not as riled up. If anything, they see the aliens and get even more riled up."

"Oh, really? The wildlife get riled up because they're aliens?"

"Well, they probably sense that they're, you know...not from here."

I rubbed my forehead. Humans weren't exactly native here, either.

I thought of telling him 'no' and that there was no way any of us would survive out there in the wild.

Setting up a settlement from scratch would be insanely tough to do, let alone when we didn't have any experienced people and resources were scarce. I thought of all that, and then some more.

But, in the end, Roddik would go ahead with it, no

matter what I said. This time, I wouldn't be able to stop him.

And so, I decided I would have to trust him.

There wasn't any choice. And if, for a moment, I thought of the electric thrill that ran through me at Iq'her's touch, well, that memory would be all I'd have of him.

"A fresh start," I whispered, and his smile widened. "Let's do it."

IQ'HER

.

I could survive the lumpy bed.

And the flat, too-soft pillow.

Even the scratchy blanket.

But I was tired of the nonsense, tired of the bad nights' sleeping, tired of being the only one on Strike Team Two that didn't have his own place to sleep.

I still shared a room at the bunk house simply because I had been too preoccupied to get my own place.

To be honest, I had never cared about having my own place. I didn't see the need to have one if I was rarely going to be there.

But, after the raucousness of the ground crews celebrating hitting a construction goal last night, and the horrific, twitch-inducing cooking from the man that claimed to be a cook... I needed my own place to eat and sleep.

One of the women that Vidia knew had been pushing a private domicile at me. I had grudgingly seen it a few weeks ago. It was nice. A bit big for my tastes, but it was a nice place.

The owners had been an older couple, and while they and their apartment building had survived the war intact, their son-in-law hadn't. So they'd moved, to help their daughter raise her children, leaving just days before the vines had encircled Nyheim.

In the morning, I told her I would purchase the place. She was so happy, I swore she was crying as she sent me the electronic signature sheets. An hour later, I was the proud owner of my own home.

I spent the next hour before my shift started at the warehouse where furnishings had been stored. The pickings were slim. Industry as it stood on Ankau was just beginning to ramp back up. Which meant that most stores had a mixture of pre-war goods and some shoddily manufactured cottage industry products.

But it would do for now.

I would have peace and quiet, far more important than furniture.

Because surely the only thing that had kept me awake all night was the commotion from the others.

Not thoughts of a stunning pair of eyes, sparking with temper.

Not lush, full lips, curved up slightly at the corners, tempting me.

It wasn't at all that I thought how much Stasia might like the house, where another family had lived for decades, their bonds strong and tight despite everything that had happened to them.

Not at all.

When I'd finished, Tobias greeted me with a particularly strong cup of coffee, something that I had acquired an affinity for since arriving on this planet.

"How are things in your part of the universe?" I asked.

He told me he was interested in a young lady that was one of Vidia's assistants but wasn't sure how to approach her.

"Just be honest with her," I suggested. "You are a remarkable young man with a lot of optimistic energy, and I've seen you when you get angry, so I know that you're also very capable of protecting her if needed. Just walk up to her and say 'hi'. Then go from there."

"Thank you, Iq'her. I just," he hesitated as he looked up and down the halls. "I just don't know if I can talk to her. She's so beautiful and I'm... well, I'm me."

"Seriously?" I was incredulous with disbelief. He was a handsome man, even by K'veri standards. His only real flaw was his lack of confidence. "You need to... what's the phrase... man up and talk to her. Just go to her, strike up a conversation, and be who you are. Don't lie to her, don't play games with her, and don't try to impress her by doing things you don't normally do. If she doesn't share your feelings, that means you were destined for another and she's simply scenery."

He nodded, thanked me, and returned to his work. I headed to my tiny little office to do mine. I set down my coffee on my desk and pulled up the audio files from Stasia's evening.

Don't lie to her, I'd told Tobias.

Wasn't what I was doing even worse?

I held my finger over the button that would destroy the tape, deactivate the bug and instruct it to go dormant, falling off her skin like any other fleck of fluff.

But still... Not only did I want to be sure she was safe, if her brother was involved with more serious attempts to disrupt the food supply, we needed to know about it.

I hit the play button instead.

The voices of other men filled my earpiece, and I gritted my teeth.

It would serve me right if I had to listen to Stasia spending time, personal time, with another man.

It was irrational.

It was insane.

It was unreasonable.

But it was a fact.

I wanted her for myself. And I needed to do something about it.

Soon.

For now, I would watch. Listen. And be ready to protect her if need be.

What I did end up hearing was both what I had hoped to hear and hoped not to hear. I *had* hoped that her brother would pull his head out of his collective stupidity, but in case he hadn't, I hoped I would hear something that would give us a head start against their insanity.

I was right on the second count, to a point. There was a sizeable crowd of hateful humans, larger than I had anticipated, looking to leave and start up their own settlement.

While I normally wouldn't have cared and simply said "kout it" at the idea of them leaving, right now this was a bad idea.

The Puppet Master... terrible name in my opinion... had already shown a penchant for being a bit apoplectic when it came to man-made structures. General Rouhr had put a temporary halt to construction in new areas, in order to test one of Leena and Tella's theories. These people were looking at trying to create a brand-new settlement of man-made structures off in some previously untouched part of the forest.

This was possibly the worst plan I had heard since the Xathi were finally destroyed here.

So, of course, I was unsurprised to hear that Roddik had been one of the primary proponents of the idea. It rated just a few steps below his asinine attempt to blame his sister for why the others were still locked up.

How could Stasia possibly stay so loyal to someone so undeserving? I understood that he was her brother, but there was a certain point when family just didn't count as family anymore.

How much more would he have to say or do to get her to that point?

I took a copy of the audio file to the general's office.

"Come in," he announced after I knocked on his door. I entered and he looked up from a stack of tablets on his desk. "Iq'her. Come in. What have you got for me today?" he asked almost gratefully.

I ventured to guess that the papers he was rifling through were either more reports he didn't want to read, or his speech for today's address to the populace, explaining the food crisis in detail.

"My apologies, sir. I didn't realize what time it was. I can come back after your conference," I said.

"No," he said, almost too quickly. "No, come in. I need a few minutes' break from it anyway. Sit, talk."

I handed over the copy of the audio file and he put it into his computer as I spoke. I explained to him what had happened yesterday after the arrests, telling him everything except how fantastic Stasia was.

I didn't believe it would be terribly professional of me to editorialize like that.

He looked at me through narrowed eyes. "You're monitoring people without permission now."

"Well," I started. "You see, sir, I… well, I, uh… based on the fact that the group of humans attacked one of our food delivery trucks and then proceeded to attack us and insult us even after arrest, I felt that it might be necessary to get some intel on the group in order to determine their threat level," I said quickly, adding on a "sir," at the last moment.

"Uh-huh," he grunted as he looked at me. He didn't bother to suppress his grin as he opened the audio file. His grin didn't last long. When the file stopped playing, he seemed to age another decade right before my eyes. He put his head in his hands and groaned in frustration.

As he lifted his head, he ran his hands across his head and stared at me. I could see the muscles in his arms ripple as he subconsciously flexed them before he brought his arms down. "This is…I honestly don't know how to describe it," he said. "This is about as asinine an idea as there is. They believe that we're stealing their food, now they want to move away and start over thinking it's better out there somewhere. On a planet where trees try to eat you."

I nodded. What was I supposed to say?

He stared at me, and even though I knew the anger and disappointment weren't meant for me, I could feel them emanating from him. "This could turn into a problem," he finally said.

"Yes, sir," I nodded.

He looked at me, then down to his notes, back up at me, then at the time that was displayed on a giant clock that took up a good portion of his west wall. "I don't have time to deal with this," he started.

"But we can't just let them do whatever they want, sir!" I cut in. "What if they get even more dangerous?"

"Well, if you had allowed me to finished talking," he said sternly, "I was going to say that perhaps the speech will help alleviate, or at least ease, some of their feelings and maybe calm this whole thing down."

"What if it doesn't, sir?"

"We'll figure that out when the time comes," he answered. "For now, let's answer some questions and hope that helps."

"Aye, sir. Wait," I said, stopping halfway out of my chair. "I had thought originally you were planning to discuss this with the city leaders tomorrow."

"True, but with the accidental pre-emptive announcement," he glared at his desk comm, "Vidia convinced me that the longer I wait, the worse the situation will end up being."

I followed him out of his office and joined his security detail as we headed to the public square. It was packed.

I don't think I had ever seen so many humans in one place at the same time before.

All of them concerned, anxious about the food shortage.

It wouldn't take much to spark those worries, turn it into a mob.

I could only hope Stasia was nowhere near.

STASIA

The streets had come alive.

The atmosphere was electric with anticipation, the loud chatter of the people walking down the streets was punctuated with more questions than I imagined anyone could answer.

Still, I joined the sea of people all the same, feeling more than just a little hopeful. It was the first time the aliens and the human leadership were going to address us in person, offer explanations.

I hoped good things would come out of it.

I knew most people still had questions about the vines that had imprisoned us, or even about the now-vanquished Xathi, but the food rationing system was definitely the main subject of the whispers and rumors.

If the aliens could provide the people with real answers, maybe disaster would be avoided.

The people of Nyheim weren't that prone to violence, but in some districts, tensions were already running high. The nightly gatherings at Ventil were proof of that. People were tired of being bossed around without an explanation. And empty stomachs usually made things worse...

Hopefully, all that would come to an end soon.

Roddik walked beside me with a few of his friends, and I was happy he had decided to come. Maybe an event like this would be enough to make him change his mind. It wasn't very likely, but I thought it was at least worth a shot.

"Come on, I want to watch everything up close," he said as we arrived in the main square. The place was completely packed, thousands of people gathered there, but Roddik somehow managed to cut his way through the crowd. We made it to the front after a few minutes of bumping shoulders and stepping on the feet of onlookers, and we eyed the City Hall balcony expectantly.

One of the oldest surviving buildings in the city, the City Hall overlooked the vast main square; there was a balcony on the first floor of the building, one that was traditionally used by the mayors for their inaugural speech.

Now, though, it would serve an entirely different purpose.

We had only been there for ten minutes when the balcony doors swung open. Aliens of different races strolled out from the building, and they were accompanied by a few human women. I immediately recognized Vidia, the mayor. One of the women was pregnant - rumor had it that the father was one of the aliens.

That was another topic of much debate, but I couldn't see how it was anyone's business but hers.

For a moment, my thoughts flashed to Iq'her. The thrill that had run through me at his touch.

Stop it, Stasia. You'll probably never see him again, I chided myself.

VIDIA STOOD at the front of the retinue, her face now plastered on the multiple screens spread all over the square. I looked at the giant alien next to her - General Rouhr. He was an alien, sure, but he certainly had the gravitas of a commander. He looked exactly like the kind of man you needed on your side if you were waging a war.

But we weren't waging one anymore, were we?

So why did he have a say on how things were being run?

"People of Nyheim," Vidia started, speaking into the hovering microphone in front of her, small rotating blades keeping it up in the air. "We're facing a severe crisis - one that harkens back to the dark days of the Xathi war. And it's from that position that I address you today." She made a slight pause for effect, and only then did she continue. "As you're all too aware, food has been growing scarce. The vine dome cut us off from other cities, and during that time, we went through far more of our reserves than anyone would have hoped. Now that the dome is gone, though, we face yet another problem."

A murmur went through the crowd as she said it, but Vidia's voice drowned out the chatter as it boomed through the speakers.

"We have found out that plant life across the continent is dying at an alarming rate. In the forests, in the farms - everywhere. Concerned for our already precarious food supplies, I proposed a rationing system after consultation with General Rouhr and the other city leaders on this continent. I know the situation isn't ideal, but we're doing our best to handle it. It is our belief that all this is connected to the vines that surrounded the city, but we still haven't managed to find a concrete link. The four ladies behind me—Leena, Annie, Jeneva, and Tella—have been working around the clock to find a solution. They're our foremost experts and—"

"WE DON'T GIVE A SHIT ABOUT ANY OF THAT!" Roddik suddenly bellowed.

I jumped in place as his voice exploded into the air. I turned to him, shocked, and grabbed his arm. My fingernails dug deep into his flesh, but he didn't let that stop him. "WHAT WE CARE ABOUT IS THAT THE ALIENS HAVE BEEN STEALING OUR FOOD!"

In a fraction of a second, others joined Roddik and voiced similar opinions. Vidia did her best to continue talking, but the crowd's chatter was now turning into the angry sound of a swarm of wasps.

If no one did anything, the situation would spiral out of control… fast.

"Please, everyone," Vidia said, pulling the microphone toward her. "Let's remain calm. If you have any questions, I'll be more than happy to answer them. The important thing is for us to work together to overcome this."

No one was paying attention to her.

More people had now started to shout, fists were being raised in the air, and I noticed that the guards surrounding the general were becoming antsy. I felt a lump in my throat as I noticed some of them laying their hands on their rifles, and I recognized Iq'her among them.

There was no mistaking him: his black skin glistened under the sunlight, streaks of green snaking up his forearms, and his demeanor was as serious as ever.

Knowing that someone like Iq'her was among the aliens on the balcony made me relax, just a fraction. My body just felt safe with him and I liked knowing he was around. His presence soothed me. I had the impression that he was the kind of guy that liked to think before he acted — but I still knew the situation was a dangerous one. Things could escalate quickly, and then it'd be a free-for-all.

"Let's get out of here," I growled, tightening my grip on Roddik's arm. The idiot could have started what was slowly turning into a riot, but I wouldn't let him stay here and make things worse.

Unfortunately, he seemed to have different plans.

Not saying a word, he pulled his arm free from me and turned around. He nodded at his buddies beside him, and they quickly dispersed among the crowd. Then Roddik signaled some other guys standing right behind us with a hand gesture.

And that was the moment when I realized Roddik hadn't shouted out because he was angry.

No… the whole thing had been planned ahead of time.

"What the hell are you doing, Roddik?" I shouted,

but either he didn't hear or he didn't care. Taking his backpack off, he went down on one knee and grabbed something from the inside. It looked like a small battery box, but it had a couple of miniature rotating blades attached to it.

Fearing whatever it was my brother was trying to do, I scanned the crowd as fast as I could, and realized that his accomplices were all holding similar devices. I rushed toward Roddik. In the crowd, people had already drifted between us, making a wall. I pushed people out of the way, but it was already too late.

I couldn't stop him.

"NOW!" He screamed at the top of his lungs, jamming his thumb on a button and throwing the device up into the air. The blades started spinning furiously and the damn thing floated up, joining other similar looking devices. I didn't even have the time to blink. The devices started flying toward the balcony, the aliens screamed something, and then it was chaos.

The devices exploded at random, the noise of it making my ears ring, and I held my arms up in front of my face as debris started falling over the crowd. Clouds of smoke were now shrouding the balcony where the aliens were, but I could still hear them shouting orders.

Still standing upright, my feet were glued to the ground. I was too shocked to move. I tried to see through the smoke, praying that no one had died, but I couldn't see a damn thing. If Roddik had murdered anyone, would that be my fault, as well? Had I failed so miserably as a sister that my brother had turned into a monster?

"Don't just stand there, you idiot!" Roddik screamed, and then he grabbed my wrist and pulled me after him. I wanted to slap him, to do something other than just be a helpless witness in all this, but I simply didn't have it in me.

I just let him drag me through the crowd, too confused to do or say anything.

IQ'HER

I tackled Rouhr to the ground as the first modified explosives landed. The rest of his security detail protected the women. As quickly as it had started, the attack stopped as the perpetrators ran away.

I saw, at the far end of the crowd, Stasia being dragged away by her brother. As much as I wanted to chase after them, there were fires to be put out first. Shouts of confusion and fear filled the air as the liquid explosives spread fire through the square.

"Take care of the injured," Rouhr yelled out to us as I got off him and helped him up. I nodded quickly and moved to care for an elderly woman only a few feet away. The crowd that had been there, a few thousand strong, had broken into a stampede of confusion and chaos.

Dozens were running for water while many more were trying to beat and kick the fires out. Several more were trying to deal with the wounded, and all of that within a few quick moments from the first bottle shattering open and flinging fire wherever it could.

There were calls for help, cries of pain, and shouts for lost people filling the air. Soon enough, sirens could be heard as emergency vehicles arrived to aid the personnel already there.

"What the kout happened?" I heard someone next to me shout above the chaos. Sakev knelt nearby, helping a young child that had been trampled in the panic. Her leg was at an awkward angle and he was doing his best to try to calm her as he looked at her twisted limb.

"I don't know," I answered back. "You're going to be okay, ma'am. You only have a few minor scratches," I told her.

"Thank you. Is my granddaughter okay?" Tears welled in her eyes. "She fell out of my arms when I was jostled from behind."

I made a quick comparison between the two and saw the same hair, eyes, and slightly crooked nose. "She's alive, ma'am, but I'm afraid her leg might be broken," I said quietly, directing her attention to her left.

She looked and let out a desperate cry. She crawled

over to Sakev and her granddaughter, crying and apologizing.

"Rekking bastards," he said to me. "They knew that would cause chaos, prevent us from chasing their asses down and breaking them." For someone that was supposed to be annoyingly funny, I wasn't at all surprised by his anger. I felt the same way.

After nearly half an hour, medical personnel and volunteers had taken over dealing with the wounded and finding lost children. The fires had been quickly put out and all three strike teams were gathered near where Rouhr had been standing.

Vrehx was livid, barely controlling his anger. "I want those bastards found," he growled. He hovered over Jeneva, who was *extremely* pregnant. She wiped grime from her face and patted his hand. She might be annoyed, but Vrehx was ready to kill something.

"Iq'her, Tu'ver," he said, looking at us. I hadn't realized that Tu'ver was standing right behind me. "Get into the security footage, now. Get us pictures of everyone involved. If they're still in the city, I want them in a tiny little box before they get a chance to get away."

He looked at Sylor next. "Make sure the underground gets a copy of those pictures, I don't want these rekking assholes thinking they can hide out down there."

We all nodded. The three of us, Tu'ver and I with our implants, Sylor with his modified sleeve, quickly got into the cameras. It wasn't long before every member of the strike teams had pictures of the men and women that had thrown the explosives.

"Find them," Vrehx snarled.

I found myself slightly worried for the people involved. If he found them, alone, I wasn't sure his temper would allow him to bring them back unmarked.

The teams divided, each of us armed, thanks to Tobias having guards gather our gear for us, and I went searching for Roddik and Stasia.

I knew Stasia hadn't been a part of this, she wasn't like her brother or the people on the recording, so I wanted to be the one to find her. If any of the others did, they weren't going to be as calm around her.

She might be injured.

Unacceptable.

If I had time, I could remotely access the bug on her, connect it to the grid of satellites Karzin had launched, and find her.

But right now, it was a risk. Should I take the time for the recoding, and then be able to go right for her, or chance that maybe one of the other teams would find her first.

Either way, the stakes felt too high.

I quickly fell into a search pattern, checking out the

area just north of the square. Within minutes, I saw a flicker of movement as someone ducked behind a corner. I cautiously jogged over, my assault rifle at the ready. I would have preferred to use my gloves, but an assault rifle used the right way was more likely to get people to surrender.

As I neared the corner, my quarry turned out to be Stasia and Roddik. Roddik yanked on his sister's arm to get her to follow him. "Roddik!" I yelled as I entered the alley. Even from as far away as I was, I saw his eyes go wide and he pulled on Stasia harder, causing her to wince. They ran, her stumbling behind him, face pale.

"Back off, freak!" Roddik shouted.

He wouldn't hurt her, not his own sister. Would he?

I fell back slightly, still following them, but I was unfamiliar with the backstreets and alleys in this area. When I followed them into another alley, there were nine different points of entry — or exit — for them to choose from. I looked down each little alley access, but never saw them.

I did, however, see another of the attackers trying to open a door. I rushed him, ducking his wild punch and putting my shoulder into his chest. The air whooshed from his lungs as we went to the ground. A quick tap to the side of his head with my rifle and he was disoriented enough for me to bind him.

I didn't take any chances of him managing to escape,

so I bound his hands, then his ankles, then his hands to his ankles behind him. He was uncomfortable, to say the least, but I didn't care.

I put another tracker on him so I wouldn't lose him, and continued my search for Roddik, Stasia, and anyone else I could find.

By the end of the day, I had captured three of the idiots and directed one of the vans that Team Three had commandeered to their locations. As the sun was setting, we were all back at the town square with Rouhr.

"Is Vidia okay, sir?" Daxion asked. He had been on the outskirts of the crowd when the attack happened, so he had been able to quickly round up four of the suspects before they could escape. He had even grabbed one of the 'wounded' before they could be taken to the hospital and sneak away.

All together, we had nearly a dozen people arrested, eight of those thanks to me and Dax.

Rouhr nodded. "She's fine. Tobias covered her with his own body, got a bit of a burn on his leg because of it, but he's otherwise uninjured. He's coordinating with her now on cleanup and everything else."

I looked over and saw Tobias speaking with a very cute young lady. The way he smiled at her, even when he was serious, suggested that this was the girl he had told me about. I did notice that his left pant leg was burned, but he seemed to pay it no mind. I shifted my attention back to the general.

"We need to figure out why this happened, who those people are, and if there is another attack coming," he said. "Vrehx, I want your team in charge of interrogations."

Vrehx nodded. He was barely paying attention as he stared at his communicator, presumably keeping tabs on Jeneva's condition.

Rouhr gave him a sympathetic look, turned to Tu'ver, who nodded in acknowledgement, and then turned his focus to Team Three. "Sk'lar, I want your team to coordinate with the city's police force and conduct another search. I want everyone involved with this brought in for questioning."

"Understood, sir."

With a nod, Rouhr looked at Karzin. "You and your team get the fun job, you get to go aerial and search the forest. I doubt many of them stayed in the city limits, but I also doubt most of them are smart enough to lay low before coming together."

"Understood. But…" Karzin started.

"Yes?" Rouhr asked, obviously not in the mood.

"How do we know who was involved and who was simply caught up in the rush of the chaos and trying to get out of the way? I mean," he quickly added, "for Team

Three. Anyone running and hiding in the forest is going to be part of this, obviously."

I spoke up as Rouhr pointed to me. "I have an audio recording of people planning to leave the city and create their own society, ahem, 'without aliens'. I can always do a voice comparison."

"Fine. Let's get these idiots before they cause any more harm and destruction," Karzin said.

Now that there had been time to breathe, I'd taken the opportunity to reprogram the tracker, and expanded the area of coverage.

I swore.

The tracker showed her heading out into the forest, just as Rouhr suspected. "Wait," I said, stopping my team.

"What?" Rokul demanded.

"If we go in there full-bore, it's going to create a situation where we might have to use deadly force," I said.

"And?" Rokul asked with a shrug.

"And that would be bad, brother," Takar answered as he placed his hand on his brother's shoulder. "If we are still dealing with humans that hate us, imagine how much worse the situation will become if we end up killing some."

"Fine," Rokul said angrily. "What do we do then?"

I stepped forward, turning my attention to Karzin,

noticing that Rouhr had stepped a little closer to hear. "I could use a holobelt. Infiltrate the group and get more intel. Maybe I can convince them to come back to the city, but I doubt it. But, with more intel, we can figure out a better plan to deal with this."

"I like it," Rouhr said. "However, I want you to be on the alert and ready to get out at the first sign of trouble, got it?"

I nodded. I wanted to be out there. It worried me and frustrated me to no end that I couldn't immediately go check on Stasia and make sure she was alright. I wanted to be close to her, before that insane brother of hers got her in any more trouble and put her in any greater danger.

"Fine," Rouhr said. "Do it."

STASIA

It was already night when we finally stopped.

I sat on an old tree stump, head between my knees as I tried to catch my breath. Locks of hair were plastered to my forehead; my shirt was covered in dark patches of sweat. I could barely breathe. My pants had slight tears below the knee, courtesy of the thorny plants that covered this part of the forest.

Only when my heart rate returned to normal did I dare look up.

Roddik's group of rebels and misfits was scattered across the small clearing, and they all seemed to be as exhausted as I was. For a long time, no one said anything, the only sounds reaching my ears being those of small animals scurrying away from us in the night. Roddik went on and on, several times mentioning how right he was, how the forest wasn't as dangerous as it used to be, how he had known all along.

I just rolled my eyes.

"Here," I heard Roddik say.

I looked to the side to see him standing across from me, a bottle of water in his hand.

He tossed it to me, and I grabbed it mid-flight with just one hand. Even though I was thirsty—probably more than I had ever been—I didn't open the bottle. I just sat there, my eyes on Roddik's, as anger coursed through me.

"Why didn't you tell me?" I asked him, my voice nothing but a whisper. I was struggling to keep it together, and was actually surprised I was resisting the urge to have my hands around my idiot brother's neck.

"Tell you what?" he asked, a smile on his lips. There was an amused expression on his face, one that told me I wasn't being taken seriously. That, at least, wasn't surprising.

When was the last time Roddik had taken me seriously?

"Something so stupid and dangerous," I continued, not even knowing if I was talking to him or to myself. "Why didn't you tell me you were going to do something as reckless as that?"

"I didn't tell you because you would've stopped us." Shrugging, he grabbed another bottle of water from his backpack. Opening it, he drank almost the whole bottle at once.

"Of course I would've." I raised my eyebrows. "Who in their right mind would do something like that? What exactly did you think you were going to accomplish?"

"Don't you see it?" he asked me with an air of superiority. His self-importance was almost nauseating. "I did it so the aliens would learn their lesson. It's high time they stop thinking they can walk all over humans. And I believe they got the message, loud and clear."

"You went too far." I gritted my teeth, my fingernails digging into the palms of my hands so hard I could've drawn blood. "You could've killed somebody, Roddik. In fact, you might've killed somebody. And now… we'll never be able to go back to the city."

"Who cares about Nyheim?" Turning to the side, he gestured toward the horizon line. "We're going to build our own settlement. We're going to have the fresh start we dreamed about, Stasia, away from all those who think they can rule us. Here, we'll be free."

"You have it all figured out, don't you?" I cried out, jumping up to my feet.

He didn't even flinch. Holding my gaze, he kept that smug smile on his face, almost as if he were dealing with a tantrum thrown by a petulant child.

"Roddik Cole, the brave leader of the rebels, genius of the revolution. Is that how you see yourself?"

"I don't want to be a leader," he said. For a moment, I almost believed him. "I just want to do what's best for the people."

"Yeah? Well, the people," I insisted, gesturing toward the group, "are expecting you to lead them. And if you really want what's best for them, you better rise to the challenge. None of us can return to the city, so you better make this work."

"It will work, Stasia. Why don't you just trust me?"

"Because I don't believe you've thought any of this through." Shaking my head, I sat back down on the tree stump, already feeling a headache brewing behind my eyes. Just what I needed. Pinching the bridge of my nose, I let out an audible sigh. "What are we going to eat, Roddik? Have you thought about that?"

"We can forage, and some of us know how to hunt."

"What about the other supplies we're going to need? How exactly are we going to build a settlement now that we're pariahs? It's not like you can send someone back to Nyheim with a shopping list, you know?"

"You worry too damn much, Stasia," he said, sighing in a manner that had me thinking he was trying to mimic me.

I didn't know if that was on purpose or not, but his attitude was leaving me even more frustrated. I felt like tearing my hair out.

"We have everything we need right here. We'll start

by using the forest to our advantage, then we can figure something out with the rest of the settlements where the aliens don't have a presence. We won't need Nyheim... or those damn aliens."

"Whatever you say," I breathed out. I wasn't in the mood for another fight, not in the situation we were in. And as much as I didn't want to be a part of any of it, I had to keep my head on my shoulders. Our lives depended on it. "What's the plan now?" I asked, looking up at him. "Are we going to camp here for the night?"

"We are." He nodded, hands on his hips as he watched the group unpack. I followed his gaze and, for a moment, said nothing. Most people had brought some backpacks with them, probably the only thing they managed to carry during our hasty escape, but no one seemed to have brought any kind of camping supplies.

There wasn't a single tent in sight.

"Is this everyone?" I continued, doing my best to come to terms with the situation. "Or are we waiting for more people to join us?"

"No, this is it," he replied. For the first time since our conversation started, I noticed a shadow in his smile. "There were supposed to be more of us, but I figure not everyone managed to get out of the city. Some must've been captured during our escape."

"You don't seem particularly concerned."

"Should I be?" He shrugged. "If we're going to do this right, we can't worry about those weak and stupid enough to be caught. The ones that didn't make it here… well, maybe they didn't deserve to be here in the first place."

"Now that's a real leader talking," I scoffed, barely believing what he was saying. "Don't let the others hear any of that bullshit, or else they'll tear you to pieces." I stood up then, ready to walk away, but couldn't resist throwing Roddik one final snide remark. "Not that you don't deserve a beating."

With that, I stalked away from him and headed toward the group. People were starting to cluster in small groups, and I tried to make a mental inventory of what everyone had brought. There were some cooking utensils, and everyone seemed to have brought whatever food they had at home. Not that it meant much — judging from what I was seeing, we'd be out of food in a couple of days. But that wasn't my main concern for the night: aside from some blankets, no one really seemed that ready for a night outside.

I groaned inwardly as I realized that a few pans and blankets were all that we had. If Roddik thought we'd be able to build a settlement out of that, he was in for a rude awakening.

I doubted we'd be able to survive for more than a couple of weeks.

To make matters worse, I hadn't brought anything with me. Roddik had kept me in the dark before this, and that meant I hadn't packed a damn thing. Thankfully, he had packed a bag for me before we left, so at least I had a blanket and whatever clothing he had managed to cram in there.

It would still be a long, cold night, no doubt about that.

For a moment, I thought of helping Roddik out. Maybe I could organize something with the group. We desperately needed to know what kind of skills everyone had and leverage that for our advantage before it was too late.

"But that's not happening tonight," I muttered under my breath, raking one hand down my face. My head hurt like hell, and I was still feeling exhausted from all those hours of running. Maybe I'd be able to help the group, but that would have to wait.

With a blanket under my arm, I moved away from the group and toward the edge of the clearing. Roddik was now happily chattering with everyone, and I simply couldn't stand his presence. Somehow, I didn't feel as if Roddik was still my brother. It felt as if he was...a stranger.

Even if only for the night, I needed to be by myself.

My life had changed, after all, and I still hadn't processed any of that.

Finding what I hoped was a good spot to lay my blanket on the ground, I curled up against a tree trunk and closed my eyes. With my jacket thrown over my torso, I tried not to think of the cold and focused on the gentle rustling of the leaves in the wind.

My mind drifted back to the life I'd had in Nyheim, and I sighed as I accepted that the life I used to have was now more than gone. After all, I was pretty certain that the government would think I had been an accomplice in the attack.

I had no choice: I would have to survive here.

I thought about Iq'her. He'd never believe I wasn't a part of this. He'd think I was one of Roddik's loony followers. He'd never touch me again.

He'd never hold me.

I'd never feel that thrill at his touch again.

Never.

IQ'HER

If I was going to infiltrate this group of humans, I was going to need gear and tech that was decidedly human. I headed to the guards' storehouse and raided their equipment.

I didn't gather much, but enough to make myself seem useful to Roddik's group of malcontents. It had been one night already that Stasia had been in the forest. I was worried about her.

I was beyond angry at Roddik for placing her in this danger.

I grabbed a small, ordinary tablet loaded with maps and a couple of flashlights, stuffed them all into a bag with a couple spare changes of clothes, and made my way to my office. In there, I stored all my gear, including my sleeve... which hurt more than I had anticipated, emotionally speaking...and grabbed the only three pieces of K'ver tech that I was willing to risk taking.

I put on my holobelt, quickly entered in a disguise, and turned it on. With the Xathi war on Ankau, neither I nor Tu'ver had ever gotten the chance to fix the holobelts to be more stable during hand-to-hand combat. But it would have to do for now.

The sensation I felt was... nothing. The holobelt did absolutely nothing to us physically that we could actually feel. All it did was project a holographic disguise over our bodies. The distance between the disguise and our real skin was less than one-quarter the depth of skin, so it was about as impossible to see through as reality was.

The second piece of my own personal tech that I'd grabbed was the small tracker that I needed to follow and find Stasia's signal. The plan was to follow the signal until I found the group, bury the tracker so that it couldn't be found on me if I was searched, and make myself known to the group. Hopefully, I would be able to convince them that I was one of them and then I could slowly get information.

The third... well, I'd hope it stayed hidden and unused. It didn't look like much, wouldn't look like anything to unknowing eyes.

My tracking bugs were one-way only,

unfortunately. I wouldn't be able to use it to both send information to Rouhr and receive orders. The tracker and holobelt would already be a risk.

I'd have to chance finding a human comm unit with Roddik's group and modifying it.

I headed out of my office and went to a nearby cleansing room—or bathroom, as Tobias insisted on calling it, despite it not having a bath in it. Humans.

I looked at myself in the mirror and was unhappy with the disguise it had picked. I quickly made some alterations to the disguise, settling on one where my normally bald head was covered in dark hair, my black eyes were more human-shaped, and I had a deep tan.

Satisfied with my choice, I went back to the warehouse I'd visited just a few days before, when furnishing a home had seemed the most pressing issue.

I looked around with new eyes. Any of the homes or apartments that remained empty due to the occupants never coming back had been cleaned out and their items brought to the warehouse where they were cleaned, categorized, and labeled. If any of the previous occupants did return to Nyheim, they were brought here to retrieve their possessions.

The possessions of those unable to return were later resold or used for the communal good.

It was to this section of the warehouse that I headed. I grabbed another bag, something that looked well used, and put in whatever gear I thought I could get away with as camping supplies.

I grabbed two blankets, a sleeping bag, a small three-person tent, a cooking stove and some fuel, and some rope. I then grabbed a hatchet, two hunting knives, and a small pot and pan set along with a plate, a cup, and a set of eating utensils.

Everything was carefully organized and packed into the large duffel bag and strapped across my shoulders, just above the other pack that I had with my clothes and tech. I tested my movement, made a small adjustment, tested it again, and I was finally satisfied with it.

All I needed was another old looking bag, something I could tie to my hip. I looked around, spending more time than I liked searching before I finally found one. It looked much newer than I preferred, but I could always claim that it had been purchased recently to replace an older, broken one.

I left the warehouse, went to a market, purchased a small amount of food, and put it into the small bag. Finally set up, I made my way out of the city and slowly into the surrounding forest. Using the tracker, I continued to head northwest, in the direction of Vidia's old city of Fraga.

I walked for nearly three hours, the thin light creating long shadows through the trees, before I finally started to get close. The tiny beacon on the tracker was suddenly bright. That meant that I was within a mile of the bug I had placed on Stasia's neck.

I slowed my walk, taking my time. I had to keep one eye on the forest floor, one eye out for rogue plants trying to kill me, and one eye out for any possible lookouts that the humans had put out.

I understood that that meant I needed three eyes, but I was reasonably confident that the humans hadn't put anyone out as a lookout. This entire enterprise didn't seem to be well thought out enough to provide for lookouts and patrols.

Maybe one or two of the humans would have thought of it. I'm sure Stasia would have if she was running it. But with Roddik in apparent control... I highly doubted that he had thought that far ahead. Once again, I worried about Stasia. I didn't know what dangers she was facing.

With a shake of my head, I put my worries out of my mind. I'd see her soon enough and then she would be fine.

And if she was harmed...then I would have vengeance on her brother.

To be honest, it seemed unlikely that Roddik had thought very far ahead at all. I was willing to bet they were going to set up a temporary camp for tonight, then try to get as far away from Nyheim as possible in the morning before trying to find a place to create their new 'settlement'.

If I had been running this, I would have already had people setting up a campsite, ensuring that there were supplies and gear ready. Then, with a map and a definitive direction and location in mind, we would have headed out, resting a few hours in the evening and morning, walking the rest of the time to ensure that we would be able to get away from Nyheim and any pursuers.

As the tracker began to blink brightly, telling me that I was only a few hundred yards away, I ducked down behind a large tree and dug a hole. I put the tracker into the hole, covered it, and stood up.

After a deep breath, I started walking again. I was wary of my surroundings, yet nothing moved towards me, or even away from me. I knew that not all the plants and trees were sentient and mobile, but I also remembered back to when we were dealing with the Xathi. This part of the forest had been teeming with life, and we had been forced to defend ourselves multiple times from trees that whipped at us and animals that tried to stab us or poison us with their hooves.

Now, there was nothing. It could have been due to the large number of humans that had come rushing through here. It could also have been because the

Puppet Master killed off the vegetation. Thinking about that, I stopped and studied some of the trees around me in the pale light. They looked healthy, as did the vegetation on the forest floor.

That was odd. Why was this untouched when so much more was dying?

I moved on, knowing that I wasn't going to answer that question tonight.

It wasn't long before I came upon the campsite. There weren't as many people there as I expected. This was even more of a haphazard venture than I had thought.

I slowly made my way through the trees, making sure to step on a few branches as I did so to alert them that I was near. As I stepped into the small clearing they had chosen, Roddik and four of his people advanced on me.

"Hi," I said innocently, even waving as I came in sight.

I don't think I did that right. Two of Roddik's friends grabbed me forcefully. I resisted. I didn't resist terribly hard, but I didn't want to look like a complete pushover, either.

"Hey, hey! Let me go," I cried as I shrugged out of their grips, pushing the one to my left. The one on my right punched me, a decent blow that caught me on the side of the head. I stumbled back, selling the moment a bit, and swung at him, making sure to pull my punch a bit.

It was a solid connection with his nose. Blood spurted out as he let out a yell and grabbed at it. The one that I'd pushed kicked at me, catching me in the leg. It was a solid kick, knocking my leg out from under me. I dropped to one knee, blocked his punch, then... as Roddik and the other two advanced, I let him hit me again.

I started pleading with them, yelling out that I was there to help. One of them caught me in the face with a fist. I could feel the blood starting to well up at the top of my nose. I could stop the bleeding, but I snorted in order to make it bleed more.

I kicked out and struggled, but not enough to break free when they grabbed me again.

"You made a mistake," Roddik said as he walked up and punched me in the jaw. I gathered he meant for the punch to knock me unconscious — he had certainly watched too many human movies — so I pretended to be dazed and barely hanging on.

"Tie him up," he ordered the others. "And can someone tell me where the fuck my sister is?"

My mind reeled.

Why was Stasia missing?

For the first time in a long time...I was afraid.

STASIA

I woke up startled.

Even though I had kept some distance from the group, I was close enough to hear all the shouting in the clearing. I sat up immediately, ears perked up as I tried to process the shouting and turn it into discernible words. My first thought was that the aliens had found us. It wouldn't have been hard for them to follow after us, and now I feared a massacre. Roddik had acted like a terrorist, and I wouldn't have been surprised if a strike team simply rappelled down from a shuttle into the clearing and opened fire.

"Crap," I muttered as I jumped to my feet.

Before I even knew what I was doing, I was rushing through the forest toward the clearing. Twigs and branches whipped at my arms and face, but I didn't let that stop me. As much as I hated what my brother and his friends had done, I couldn't stand aside and let them be gunned down.

"Roddik!" I cried out the moment I saw some shadowy figures in the distance. Without even caring if they were humans or aliens, I just made my way toward them as fast as I could. "What the…?"

There were no aliens to be seen there. Aside from Roddik and a few of his friends, the only newcomer was a man I had never seen before. His skin was tanned, and he had black eyes and hair as dark as a raven's feather. He didn't seem to be much older than me, but there was something about him that made it difficult to pinpoint his age.

Also, he had been tied to the base of a tree.

Blood trickled down slowly from his nose, but he didn't seem particularly concerned with that. Even though Roddik was cracking his knuckles right in front of him, almost as if he was readying himself for another punch, the stranger seemed completely relaxed.

"What the hell's going on?" I asked, still struggling for air. Adrenaline had made me faster, but my lungs were still recuperating from the mad dash I had done on our way here. "Who is this?"

"He's an intruder," Roddik said with a frown. His friends simply followed his lead and nodded their agreement, none of them bothering with looking me in the eyes. "We caught him trying to sneak into the camp."

"I wasn't trying to sneak," the stranger finally spoke up. "I greeted you and announced myself. Would I have done that if I wanted to cause any trouble? The only thing I want is to join you."

There was something about how this man carried himself that was so familiar, something about how he spoke that made me think I knew him. But every time I tried to think about it, Roddik spoke and ruined any thoughts I was having with his inane chatter.

"You want to join us?" My brother echoed, surprise stamped on his face. It seemed that even he couldn't help but be surprised people would consider flocking to his cause.

I didn't blame him — the fact someone was actively trying to join us without having taken part in the attack had me completely floored.

Just how dumb was this new guy?

"Why the hell do you want to join us?" I asked him, taking a step forward. I glanced down at him, looking straight into his eyes, but couldn't read his expression. There was something off about this guy, but I couldn't really tell what it was.

"It's simple," the man shrugged. "Life isn't the same after the aliens' arrival. People have died, and we're never given the whole story. The way I see it, it's only a matter of time until Nyheim falls. The rational thing to do was to join a group like yours. I believe that I'll have the best chance at survival if I'm around like-minded people."

Once more, I had that feeling that something was off about him. His arguments were rational and calculated, and while they aligned with everything my brother liked to espouse ... they simply didn't seem to fit with the man's whole demeanor.

Why would a rational guy join a group that was being chased down by the authorities?

Why take the risk?

"I don't buy it," Roddik said, voicing my suspicions. "What's your name?"

"The name's Ilkay."

"And how did you manage to find us, Ilkay?"

My brother lowered himself so that his eyes were level with Ilkay's. "After the attack, I realized that someone must had coordinated the whole thing. I found a group that was leaving town to join up with you, but those damn aliens came and arrested everyone. Somehow, I managed to escape. I was alone, but I wasn't about to stay in Nyheim and let the aliens lay their hands on me. And so I set out by myself, just walking in the direction the group I was with said you'd go."

"And you just came across us?"

"I spent the whole night wandering." Ilkay shrugged, some emotion finally showing in his face. What emotion it was, I couldn't say. "I wasn't sure how much of a head start you had, so I figured I should just keep walking instead of camping out for the night. I thought that, with some luck, I'd come across you. And now, here we are."

"Here we are indeed," Roddik repeated, and I could tell he was weighing his options. He wasn't entirely sure if he trusted the newcomer, but I knew he was intrigued about the possibility of having one more person in the group admiring him. His ego was growing with each hour that passed, it seemed.

"Check my bags." Ilkay pointed with his chin to the bags laid on the ground just a few feet away from him. In direct contrast with the rest of our group, this guy seemed to have come prepared. Just one look at his bags and I immediately spotted a sleeping bag and what looked like a foldable tent.

When Roddik turned the bags over, dozens of cans of foods tumbled onto the ground. From meat to dried vegetables, this guy seemed to have come prepared for a long time in the wild. In his other bags were his camping gear, a few clothes, and the kind of tools a sensible person would have brought on such an expedition.

I wasn't sure if I trusted this new guy, especially

because he seemed to agree with Roddik's stupid reasons, but I did respect the fact that he had come prepared. Our little group desperately needed people with common sense, no doubt about that.

"Not bad," Roddik nodded with a satisfied smile, his eyes taking in the various tools and food Ilkay had brought with him.

In the grand scheme of things, the fact one man had remembered to bring a few tools wouldn't make a difference, but we weren't in a position to turn our nose up at him. "Ilkay, I've decided you can stay."

"Thank you," Ilkay replied happily, rubbing his wrists when Roddik's men finally untied him. Standing up, he stretched his back and shook Roddik's hand. "I'm looking forward to helping around here. What do you need me to do?"

"Well, uh," Roddik stammered, and it was more than obvious that he had no plan. For a guy whose sole purpose was to lead us, he seemed completely unprepared for it.

Gritting my teeth, I realized I would have to fill in for him.

"The plan remains the same, right?" I asked, turning to Roddik. I hated the fact I had to pretend my ideas were Roddik's, but I didn't want him to shoot me down just because he wanted to assert himself in front of his friends. "You said we should build a temporary site here, so I figure we should start gathering some wood for the structures."

"Right, exactly," Roddik said, a grandiose expression on his face. It seemed as if he didn't mind taking credit for my ideas. I didn't mind either — the important thing was the group's survival. "That's the plan."

The first light of dawn crept through the trees. Roddik looked around, face stern.

"Then let's get to work."

IQ'HER

Working with the group wasn't as much of an ordeal as I'd thought it would be. Then again, I had thought that joining them would be much easier, so I guess it all balanced out.

I had been assigned the job of helping to create some temporary structures. Roddik had the brilliant idea — I was pretty confident Stasia had the idea and he took credit for it — to create a small temporary site here. "That way, when others join the cause, they can rest here before they make it to our real settlement," he had said when he started ordering people around.

As I worked, gathering branches, using my hatchet to cut down some saplings and some slightly bigger trees, I paid attention to the group at work.

I had to admit that several of them had some

legitimate survival skills. They knew how to look for the right type of wood to build with, how to take vines to use as tie-downs, and how to get the right mixture of mud and undergrowth to help strengthen the structures we were building.

The more I watched, the more I thought that they could potentially stand a chance. The problem was that they were following Roddik's orders, and that was about as stupid as you could get.

There was only room for maybe four decent-sized structures in this clearing, and by 'decent-sized', I meant structures big enough for five or six people to sleep in. We weren't talking actual homes, but one-room buildings with a dirt floor and not much protection from the elements, especially if it got cold. Roddik, however, insisted on trying to fit in a fifth structure, and then got angry when one of the structures went up where he wanted it to go, insisting that he had said he wanted it in a different place.

It was his sister that kept people calm. She organized the people into different groups with different tasks.

She had some of the bigger men go to cut down trees, while she sent another group to get vines. She then suggested that some of the shorter people work on the lower portions of each 'building' and then switch with the taller people, who would be mixing together the mud insulation.

She had done well. She had also been the only one to suggest leaving to get some food. She had told her brother that she knew where to find some nuts, berries, and fruits for them all to eat.

"I don't want any goddamn fruits and berries. I want some meat," he had yelled at her when she brought it up. "Where the hell do we find meat? Can you tell me that?"

When she shook her head, he threw his hands in the air.

"Then what fucking good are you?" He stomped away from her, calling together some of the bigger men and telling them to go hunting.

"See?" he asked, turning back to his sister. "*I* just had the men go hunt for real food, not some pansy-ass berries or nuts. What the hell were you thinking?"

"I was thinking that we needed something to eat and I know where to find some," she snapped back. "What if they come back with nothing?"

"They're the biggest, meanest guys we have. How are they coming back with nothing?" Roddik spat, shaking his head as if his sister was stupid. "God, you're stupid sometimes," he said, confirming to me that he really had no clue about anything.

My blood thundered in my ears.

How dare he speak to his sister that way? She had more sense in her hand than he did in his whole body.

I felt my fingers twitch. I wanted to uncloak my holobelt and rip this little man limb from limb with my bare hands.

But I had to keep my cover. I could not.

Not yet.

"We'll go get fruits and berries with you," a couple of the women said to Stasia. They left with her.

I continued working on the small hovel I had chosen to work on. I put together, with some help, a couple of logs and positioned them into the hole some of the others had dug. These two small logs were going to be a corner.

The nearly two dozen of us worked well, not counting Roddik, who just pissed everyone off. The whole team did a good job of digging holes and small trenches for each structure. The team cutting down logs were giving us a semi-steady flow of logs to lash together with the vines that were in ready supply.

These people might actually be capable of surviving and creating a new settlement, but I wouldn't put money on it.

It was hard work, but oddly, I found myself enjoying it. For the next several hours, we worked hard and at a pretty good pace. However, things started to slow down towards the afternoon when we hadn't eaten anything.

The women had come back with a small supply of fruits, nuts, and berries.

Roddik laughed at them. "You call this finding food?" he asked as he got into his sister's face. "Really?"

She glared at him, but kept quiet.

"Figures you'd be useless out here," he said. "Now get over there and help get the buildings up. You've slacked off enough."

How she didn't yell at him, punch him in the face, or whatever to defend herself was beyond me. I could see some of the others already starting to glare at Roddik or shake their heads in sympathy towards Stasia.

They knew the siblings better than I did. They must have seen this sort of behavior before.

Stasia came to work next to me, helping me lash the logs together. We worked in silence, but every nerve of my being was attuned to her presence. I could smell her scent. I could hear her.

From time to time, I snuck a glance to admire her. She caught my eyes once but I looked away when I thought I saw the beginnings of recognition. She let it go and I concentrated on work.

The logs we were working on now were going to go up top to act as a roof, and they were the last two we needed. She tugged the vines nice and tight, tied them off, and I helped the men hoist them up and onto the hovel. They shifted slightly, but held. A couple of the smaller people got onto the shoulders of the stronger ones and lashed the roof together nice and tight. Then they began throwing some mud and sod onto the roof to help fill in the holes. It wouldn't be rain-tight, but the roof, along with the tree canopy above, should help to keep most of the rain away.

"You people should have done better," Roddik called out to us. "We've only gotten two buildings up and I wanted at least four. This is pathetic."

One of the others called him out. "Well, if you had helped, we might have gotten another one finished."

"Who said that?" Roddik yelled, spittle flying from his mouth as the crazy in his eyes was apparent.

This one is absolutely out of his mind, I thought as I stood there. I risked a sidelong glance at the person that had spoken. It was one of the men that had started the day at Roddik's side but ended the day trying to stay away from him.

No one answered him. He fumed for a minute before the hunters returned...empty-handed. "What do you mean 'there was nothing out there'?" he yelled. He started cursing and flinging blame around at 'those goddamn alien fuckers'.

The women that had gone with Stasia volunteered to go back for more fruits and nuts, taking a few extra people with them before Roddik could yell at them. I went to go sit down against a tree, and 'accidentally' picked one close to Stasia and Roddik.

"We should have spent more time planning this," I heard Stasia say as calmly as she could.

"What good would that have done?" Roddik snapped.

I heard Stasia let out a sigh and imagined seeing her breathe to regain her composure. "If we had put together a proper plan, one that used some patience and took some time, we could have already had this place built and stocked, or at least we would have had packs ready for everyone to grab on their way out of the city. Then we would have food and drink right now."

Well, we did have drink. There was a small stream only a few yards from the clearing with nice, crisp, clean water. Too bad the stream was too small to have fish in it.

"Whatever. If people just did their damn jobs and these damn aliens weren't stealing our food, this wouldn't be a damn problem." A rock flew past me and I imagined Roddik being more of a petulant child than a frustrated adult.

"Yeah, you keep saying that," she said. "But, if we had a better plan, we *would* be able to work better together and we would have gotten more accomplished."

She was right. I'd had the exact same thoughts earlier.

For me, this was yet more proof that Stasia wasn't involved in the attack on Rouhr.

She was just dragged along due to some overarching need to be loyal to her family.

He didn't deserve her loyalty. He certainly didn't deserve her love anymore. He treated her terribly and my hand itched to strike back in her defense.

No one deserved to be treated the way he treated his own family.

There had to be a way to get Stasia away from Roddik.

She deserved to live a life that didn't involve cleaning up her brother's shit.

And I intended to make sure she had that life. That she had everything she wanted.

Kneeling on the ground, I used the hatchet in my hands to hack at the bush in front of me. Arkadian berries usually hid deep inside these thorny bushes, and they were a staple of the dry season. If I was going to find any food, these berries were my best shot. I had already found some a few hours ago, but I still needed way more.

"Great," I sighed as I saw the few berries that hadn't fallen to the ground. Instead of a deep red, they were more of a sickly brown. I plucked one and it simply crumbled to dust under my fingers. It seemed like General Rouhr had been telling the truth — plant life around the city seemed to be dying.

More than that, I couldn't help but notice how few of the small animals that had always inhabited this part of the forest remained. Maybe it was because they couldn't find as much food to forage, but whatever the reason, even the animals were abandoning this place.

Defeated, I got to my feet and started making my way back toward the camp. I'd already known that foraging wouldn't be easy, but I never imagined I would be returning with nothing but a couple of berries. The situation was even more worrying than I had thought initially. The food we had brought with us wouldn't last long, so we desperately needed to find a way to keep ourselves fed.

"No luck, huh?" I heard someone ask me, right when I reached the clearing, and I turned around to see Ilkay looking at me. He was a tall man, and his strong frame had given him a semblance of respect among the other men in the group...still, there was a kindness in his eyes I hadn't expected from someone that introduced himself as an alien-hater. It struck me as familiar.

It couldn't be...

Could it?

"No," I sighed.

"Nothing?" Ilkay asked.

"The ecosystem is all out of whack."

"It is," he nodded. "Even the animals seem to have started moving on. Even game will be scarce."

"So, you noticed, too." Running one hand through my hair, I wondered how much time it would take before the others would start noticing it, as well. Would they rebel against Roddik? Would they want to return to Nyheim? That'd be an ironic ending for this situation, no doubt about it. Especially because none of us could return, even if we wanted to.

"Aren't you going to join them?" Ilkay asked me, pointing toward the fire my brother had lit in the middle of the clearing. He and his friends had dragged a few tree stumps there, and they were sitting close to the fire while going through our food reserves.

"I don't think so," I replied. "I'm not in the mood for a night of alien-bashing rants."

"I see," he whispered. "Well, as far as I'm concerned, not all aliens are bad. I do get where Roddik's coming from, although his views might be a bit extreme."

"You think?" I snorted, raising both eyebrows as I looked at him. Why was he telling me all this? He had seemed like a regular alien-hating apologist when he was trying to convince my brother to untie him, but now…

"What are you really doing here, Ilkay?" I couldn't stop myself from asking him. Still looking at him, I pointed toward the group where my brother was. "You're not like them. You're a smart guy. So why in the world would you want to join us?" I met his gaze and held it, and there was something… something about him that I liked.

"Maybe I thought you needed some help," he said.

I simply replied with a nod, not knowing what else to say, and then Ilkay turned around and headed toward the group. I watched him go, not knowing what to make of him. He didn't seem to be a bad person, but I couldn't help but feel he wasn't telling us the whole truth. There was more to him than met the eye.

Sighing, I tried to clear my head.

Why was I worrying about one guy when this whole thing was a mess? Ilkay was the least of my problems. Shaking my head, I moved away from the group and went toward the edge of the clearing. The shadows were growing long, and the sun had already started dipping over the horizon. Soon enough it'd grow cold, and I needed a fire of my own. Sure, I could share a fire with Roddik and the guys, but I preferred my own company.

I gathered a few twigs and some dry moss and, after digging a small hole, I use a lighter to get the fire going. A few minutes later and the flames were already reaching high, the sound of crackling wood making me smile. I built a small shelter with a few branches, nothing more than a basic lean-to, and then sat close to the fire as I observed the group.

Aside from Roddik's fire, there were a few others on the edge of the clearing. Most people were chattering happily, a few deep laughs drifting into the air from time to time. Everyone seemed happy with their newly acquired sense of freedom, but I couldn't stop myself from wondering about what lay ahead. There was no doubt in my mind that things would soon start going downhill. The idiots weren't even rationing their food.

"You're screwed, Stasia," I said out loud, closing my eyes as I leaned back. Roddik's settlement was nothing but a pipedream, and this group would meet a tragic end. I could help them, sure, but could I stop them being a band of idiots? I seriously doubted that. In the end, Roddik's plan was doomed and there was nothing I could do about that.

Maybe I could still save myself, though.

I could sneak away during the night...

There was no way I could go back into Nyheim, so I discarded that option right away. The moment I stepped foot inside the capital city, I was pretty sure I'd get arrested and processed as one of Roddik's accomplices. And, in a way, wasn't I one? I had escaped the city with him, after all, and I was living among his ragtag group of rebels. There was no way in hell anyone would believe me if I tried to say I wasn't a part of my brother's plans.

Nyheim was out, but maybe I could head toward one of the smaller settlements.

I could blend in and start a new life there. With the way things were nowadays, I doubted that the smaller settlements would have any kind of reliable broadcast system...and that meant they probably wouldn't have heard of the attack on General Rouhr. To them, I'd be just another faceless drifter. I'd use a different name, and no one would ever know about my past.

"Are you the lead strategist?" I heard someone say, and I raised my eyes to meet Ilkay's gaze. He stood right in front of the fire I had built, a kind smile on his lips.

"Lead strategist?" I asked, not sure what he meant.

"You just look like you're thinking hard," he continued, stepping around the fire to sit beside me. "I noticed you're one of the few thinking in practical terms around here, so I figured you were thinking about what our next move is going to be."

"Our next move?" I snorted. "Let's not die of starvation. How's that for a next move?"

"It's a reasonable one," he replied, his voice completely neutral. This guy was so damn hard to read. He was agreeable to a fault, but I never knew what the hell he was *really* thinking.

"Reasonable but difficult," I sighed. "No one's rationing their food, and food is scarce around these parts. There are no small animals we can hunt, and even the edible plants seem to have withered away. It won't take long before we're starving."

"Let's just try and not starve today," he smiled, and then produced a small packet of camping rations from inside one pocket. He threw it to me and I grabbed it midair, surprised. "I was saving that one for myself, but I noticed you still haven't eaten anything..."

"Thank you," I whispered, still looking down at the food in my hands. Hesitantly, I tore the wrapper apart and took a small bite of what looked like a protein bar, my stomach growling happily.

"Don't mention it." Holding his hands up to the fire, his eyes focused on the dancing flames, he waited a moment before continuing. "Don't let fear get the best of you, Stasia. The situation might look like a hopeless one, but there's always help to be found - even when you don't expect it."

With that, he stood up and left.

I watched him head toward his small shelter on the other side of the clearing, feeling even more confused about him than I was before. Ilkay was a strange one, but I was starting to like him.

Smiling, I lay down and rested my cheek on my hands.

A few seconds later and I was fast asleep.

IQ'HER

When the camp woke up the next morning, the people that had slept in the 'buildings' complained about the bug bites they had. Meanwhile, the ones that had slept under the lean-tos complained about the cold and how sore they were.

My first thought was about Stasia.

Was she safe?

Did she keep warm overnight?

Roddik's rabble were irritable, and with no food to eat, they were going to be even more so. I noticed that the plants around us were beginning to become even browner, odd for the middle of a wet summer. That meant there would be less food and more anger and stupid decisions.

Several of the group had their hands on their

weapons, angry at everything that was being said. While they had had no plans, and no clue, for how to survive in the wilderness on extremely limited supplies, they certainly had enough weapons to spare. Almost every one of them had a knife of some sort strapped to their hip, others had a second knife strapped to their thigh.

The axes and hatchets we had used yesterday were certainly sharp, and they had proven they knew how to use them. Finally, a quick look around at everyone prepping to move out showed that nearly two-thirds of the group were armed with rifles and handguns.

Whatever they lacked in the ability to plan, they made up for in the ability to shoot, cut, or stab.

"Uh, does anyone have an issue if I go out and look for some food? I might get lucky," I said loudly.

"Do whatever you want, but if you do find food, you better bring it back for all of us. Got it?" Roddik said, his hand resting on the butt of the gun at his hip. I knew he was trying to be threatening, and I had a feeling that of his 'many' talents, he really did know how to shoot and would be quick on the trigger if I pissed him off.

I held up my hands. "Of course, of course. I wouldn't dream of keeping anything to myself." I grabbed my pack and looked over at Stasia. "Want to come with me?" I asked. "You found the nuts and berries yesterday, so maybe you could help me find more food."

She agreed without a look at her brother.

I had to get news to Rouhr about this group. They were going to be trouble. Some people say that a rebel with a plan was dangerous, but even worse was a group of people with no plan. They would resort to a mob mentality, following the one with the loudest voice, no matter how idiotic their ideas were.

And this mob had enough weapons to seriously hurt some people. I had to find a way to get them back to Nyheim to be placed under guard, and if I couldn't do that, I had to tell Rouhr and get Stasia out of here.

However, in order to do that, I would need help. I was certain I could count on Stasia, but what if she didn't help? What if she was too afraid of betraying her brother that she didn't help me, she helped him. No, she wasn't going to be that dumb. She loved her brother, yes, but I was pretty confident that she loved her brother enough to make the right decision. To protect him from himself, she would help me.

I hoped.

I felt another wave of guilt for placing the tracker on Stasia without her knowing. But these were desperate measures for desperate times, I told myself.

After we traveled for a few miles, she finally stopped

me. "This is where we found the little bit of food," she told me, her hand grazing mine as she pointed.

Her fingers lingered on mine for just a second longer, and we shared a glance for a moment. She looked at me and I was lost in her gaze.

I wanted nothing more than to touch her, to caress her and kiss her.

"Do we know each other?" she asked, her brows drawn together.

"I would never forget you," I answered, hoping it would be enough for the moment.

I looked around. Whatever she had found must have been all that was left. This portion of the forest was nearly dead. The trees had no leaves and were starting to turn gray. The undergrowth and bushes were brown and dry. I touched one of the bushes and the leaves crumbled beneath my touch.

"It wasn't this bad yesterday," she whispered in awe. I looked at her and saw the fear and recognition of what was happening grow. "This is terrible."

"It is." I put a hand on her shoulder, and Stasia put her hand on top of mine. I gripped her and she looked at me.

Her eyes widened.

"This is crazy," she muttered to herself. It's as if she could see through my holobelt.

I looked around to ensure we were alone, then

listened carefully. There were no suspicious sounds, so I made a decision and decided it was time to take a calculated risk. "Can I show you something and have you not say anything about it?"

"You mean," she started as she looked at me, an eyebrow raised. "Like keeping a secret?"

I nodded.

She did a one-shoulder shrug. "Yes. I'm actually pretty good at secrets."

"Good." I said. I took a breath, then reached down to my belt, dropping my hand from hers. Her fingers trailed over me for a moment and I was shocked at how much I liked the touch.

I worried for one moment how she'd receive me once she saw me. But then I shrugged mentally and turned my holobelt off. When recognition dawned on her face, I turned it back on. Didn't want to risk someone following us and seeing me in my real form.

"You...you're..." she stuttered, stepping closer to me. Closer. Not away.

"I am." I brushed a stray hair from her face, let my fingers linger a moment longer than absolutely necessary.

"Why are you here? What was that? How are you able to look like that?" she rambled off quickly. Then, something inside her seemed to go off and her eyes went wider. "Are you here to kill my brother?"

I put my hand on her shoulder again and rubbed. "First, I'm not here to kill your brother. Or you," I quickly added in case she started thinking that. "This is my holobelt, it emits a holographic image on the surface of my skin in order to disguise how I look.

"As for why I'm here… I'm here to stop your brother and the rest of the group from doing anything that will result in people getting hurt, to monitor the situation, keep things from getting out of hand. I don't think this settlement idea of his is going to go the way he wants it to," I explained.

"I don't think so, either. How do you plan on stopping them?" She turned, but didn't move my hand away.

So far, she was taking my disguise in stride. That was a good sign.

"I haven't gotten around to that part of the plan yet. I was trying to gather some intel first, but with everyone pulling out their weapons, they're far too well-armed to be left to their own devices."

"Oh." She looked into my eyes again. I could see in her face that she had hoped I already had a plan in place. Then she started to get a questioning look in her eyes. "How did you find us?" Her hand pulled my hand off her shoulder. "And don't tell me you just followed behind us. If I know anything about how you guys work, you took care of the injured first. That means we had a lot of time to get away."

I opened my mouth to answer, then closed it. Guilt wracked me. To lie to her again would not be smart. So I didn't. I closed more of the distance between us again. "Do you remember when we ran into one another at the restaurant and I put my hand on your shoulder?"

"Yes," she said slowly, then bit her lower lip.

"I placed a small tracking device on your neck that allowed me to pinpoint your location after you left the city," I said quickly.

She took it well, as long as complete anger and betrayal were what you were hoping for in a reaction.

"You did what?!" She walked away from me, running her hands through her hair. "You put a tracker on me?"

"Yes. I was trying to make sure you were safe," I said. It seemed to be the wrong answer.

"Safe! Safe! You thought you were keeping me safe?" she shouted. "Of all the… you… my brother has co-opted every part of my life that he possibly can. The only things that I had that were mine, truly mine, were my body, my mind, and my privacy! And you had the unmitigated gall to think you had the right to invade two of those!"

Her voice rose with every other word until she was nearly shrieking at me. I was a bit surprised at her reaction, but it actually made sense. I *had* violated her privacy, and while I didn't exactly believe that I had violated her body, I could see how she might think that.

"I'm sorry. I... I didn't think it through," I started to apologize, reaching a hand toward her but dropping it. I felt only pain as she turned away from me.

"No shit." Stasia turned away from me, avoiding my gaze.

Yeah, I deserved that. "I was only thinking about the overall safety of the citizenry and what your brother and his group might do to them. I didn't take into account how using you without permission would make you feel. I really do apologize for that. I just wanted to keep you safe."

"Whatever." Her eyes glared into mine now. "You're just as bad as my brother, trying to talk me down like that."

From her point of view, I deserved that too, but I tried once again. "I'm sorry you feel that way. I truly did not mean to make you feel like that. However, if you're willing to help me, we can hopefully shut this down before anyone gets hurt."

That sort of calmed her. I could see that she was on the same pathway of thinking as me. She wanted to stop this before people were hurt just as much as I did. "You really want to stop anyone from getting hurt?" She put her hand to my face, both to make me look at her and signaling to me that she was more trusting of me again, having taken the time to hear me out.

Asking me the truth and listening to what I said, trusting in the honesty in my words now.

I nodded. Grateful, I noted she could have good reason not to trust me, but I wanted her to.

"And you're not here to harm my brother just because he's an asshole?" Her hand dropped from my face and I wished for it back.

I smiled. "If we arrested or hurt people for being assholes, as you put it, my entire crew would have been arrested a long time ago."

She thought about what I had to say, then hit me with a determined look. "If I help you, you take that damn tracker off me, deal?"

"I'll take it off without your help," I offered. I stepped towards her, and while she seemed to be hesitant and wary of me, she let me get close. I stepped around her, found the tracker, and pulled it off, showing it to her. I slide it into my pocket, but kept the channel open.

The need for Rouhr and the rest of command to know what Roddik was up to hadn't ended.

In fact, the more time I spent with his entire group, the more worried I became.

"See?"

"Fine. I'll help, but I'm still pissed off at you for

using me like Roddik does."

I nodded in understanding, rubbing her shoulder. "I was wrong."

Stasia paused and considered me, cocking her head to the side. "If only all men could say that." A smile crept over her lips. It was like warmth reaching me from the cold.

"I'm sorry."

Her eyes widened. "I don't think most species have mastered that one." She laughed, another sound that seemed to induce a warm feeling throughout me.

I nodded, smiling at her. "Shall we gather food?"

"Yes." She hooked her arm with mine. "Not everything is dead out here."

The hope in her voice was pleasant.

I turned around to face her. "Life is what we make of it."

"Maybe it's time to make something new," she responded, her eyelids drooping.

I leaned in and pressed my lips to her forehead so quickly that perhaps she missed it, or so I thought.

But Stasia wasn't holding back now. Cupping my face, she pressed her lips against mine, closing all space between us. She parted her lips and my tongue danced over hers. We broke away quickly.

But things had changed between us.

There was more than one kind of hope present.

"Nothing," I sighed, pointing toward the withered plants in front of us. "This time of the year, before the Xathi came, there were always a lot of wild berries around...but now, look at this. Everything's dead. No wonder even the birds have left this place."

Moments earlier, I'd been foolish enough to be hopeful. Now reality threatened to bring despair.

The stolen moment of a kiss seemed lightyears away.

Had I really been foolish to kiss him? Was I destined to make bad decisions about the men in my life?

I was loath to compare Iq'her to my brother, because while I loved my brother, he was a total asshole.

I bit my lip and brought myself back to reality.

"This is not good," Iq'her agreed, hands on his hips

as he looked at the bush. Using his hatchet, he pruned the large bush in the hopes we'd find at least a couple of berries deep inside it. Of course, there were none to be found. The forest was slowly dying... and so would we, if we didn't find any food.

"This is it." I shook my head. "We're all screwed. The little food they've brought is now gone, and I doubt the other foragers are going to find anything. Even if they do, it won't be enough for all of us."

"You're right." He nodded.

Even though I didn't like the fact Iq'her had lied to me, I had to play along. If I was being honest with myself, I'd admit that part of me really wanted to trust him, too.

If Roddik found out about what he was doing... yeah, that would be a complete disaster.

And as much as I hated the fact that Iq'her had been tracking me, I wouldn't let him become another victim of my brother's insanity. Because that's what it was — pure insanity. The food reserves were gone, everyone was in a terrible mood, and soon enough it'd be chaos.

People would be at each other's throats and, if they didn't die of starvation, they'd end up killing each other. That scenario was a far cry from Roddik's promised utopia, no two ways about it.

"We must continue," Iq'her said.

I followed after him, venturing deep into the forest.

The only sound around us was that of our own footsteps, or the one coming from the dry twigs we crushed under our boots.

There were no birds in the sky, and the forest seemed to be completely devoid of animal life. It was an eerie atmosphere, like walking in a graveyard during the night, the dead your only company. No, scratch that — even a graveyard would be livelier than this forest.

Here and there, though, we somehow managed to find a couple of berries and edible roots. That was a small blessing, but I was too painfully aware it wouldn't be nearly enough. Even if we found some more, there was no way we'd feed the whole group with a handful of berries. Still, it wouldn't be long before night fell, and so we were forced to make our way back to the camp.

"Eat some," Iq'her offered, a few roots in his hand. "Your brother will probably take everything we've gathered, so you must eat before. You have to keep your strength up."

"No." I shook my head. "They're all a bunch of idiots, but I'm not going to stuff myself while they're hungry." I almost laughed at my own comment: it would be pretty much impossible to stuff myself with the few berries and roots we had found.

"You need to keep up your strength," he insisted.

"It doesn't feel right to eat while others go hungry."

"Skrell the others. It's protecting you that I care about the most."

"Still," I insisted.

Of course, there were a lot more things that didn't feel right in this situation either, and one of them was the alien walking in front of me. Even though his true appearance was masked by his holobelt, it was now obvious to me that he had been playing a role all along. His speech was too stilted, and he didn't understand some of the jargon the guys used; more than that, his behavior contrasted with that of the others. Iq'her was too solemn, and he had something the others were sorely lacking: common sense.

My thoughts were circling. Hunger, fear, and the situation itself boxed me in at every turn.

And no matter which angle I came at the problem, I only found one solution. It was hard, but I had to trust Iq'her.

I had no other choice, really, but I still didn't feel comfortable with the fact I was betraying my brother. Or that it seemed easier because something about Iq'her made me want to trust him.

But I was conspiring against my brother with one of the aliens he despised so much. He'd have a stroke if he found out.

"We're close now," Iq'her announced as we entered a small trail, one that I knew snaked through the trees toward the clearing. I followed after him in silence, but my thoughts compensated that by being too damn loud.

"Why are you doing this?" I desperately needed some more answers, or else I'd go crazy. "My brother attacked the general, and he was causing mayhem in the city. You should be hunting him down and yet... here you are, trying to make sure no one dies."

He didn't say anything for a moment, but I could tell he was trying to think of a reply. Iq'her stopped in his tracks and I almost bumped into him.

"I know your brother believes that we're the root of all evil. He thinks we're using the humans, and that we don't care about them. But that's not the truth. We care about you, Stasia, and most of us see it as our duty to protect everyone on this planet."

"You've been doing a great job," I said, my words dripping with sarcasm. My life had been a normal one, but things changed the moment their starship fell from the sky. War, hunger, death...things I never thought I'd have to face suddenly became the reality for almost everyone on the planet.

But something about the way Iq'her said that made think that not only did the aliens care for people, but this particular alien cared about one person -- me.

"You might not believe it, but it was never our intention to cause your people strife," Iq'her continued and, for the first time, I saw an inkling of emotion in his expression. And this time I knew exactly what that emotion was: sorrow. "I spent most of my adult life fighting against the Xathi. I saw how they ravaged the galaxy mercilessly, and it pains me to no end to know we were the ones that brought them here. We accept our responsibility in what happened, Stasia, but we can't change the past."

"I know that," I whispered, my heart beating slightly faster. To hear him speak of war and the Xathi… that was enough to bring back the memories I tried to keep buried. "It's just...it's so damn hard. We lost so much, Iq'her." But hearing his emotion, seeing it? Closer. Deeper. Trusting him was possible. Probable. Even almost comfortable.

"I know," he said. "Your family…?"

"Gone," I replied, looking away from him. I held my breath, wondering if I should continue, but the words were already leaving my lips before I could filter them. "We had left the city for a day trip to Duvest the day of the first attack on Nyheim. We rushed back when we heard the sirens, but the city was swarming with those things. We tried to hide in a deserted building, but one of the Xathi… it found us."

"I'm sorry, Stasia. I truly am." His hand stroked the small of my back, and I closed my eyes. Memories washed away from me, and the way he touched me made me feel understood, safe.

"My brother would've died if it weren't for my parents," I continued, now completely unable to stop the words from coming. I had kept those memories bottled up inside me for too long, and now I had to continue my story to the end... or else the memories would just keep on eating away at my sanity. "They sacrificed themselves so that my brother and I could escape. We saw some Valorni soldiers nearby, and we tried to cry for help... but they just ignored us."

"They did?" he asked, shock clear in his voice. His hand pressed tighter against my back and I couldn't help but lean into the comforting touch.

"Yeah, they did," I repeated. "But I'm not sure if they even heard us. They were fighting, shooting... most likely, they didn't even see us at all. But my brother... he took that as proof that the *Vengeance* crew didn't really care about the humans. He used to be different, you know? He was nice, helpful, and kind... but after that day, the only thing in his heart seems to be hate."

"I understand." Reaching across the space between us, Iq'her pulled me against his chest. "It'll be alright, Stasia, I promise." In his embrace, I felt close to the breaking point. Tears stung my eyes, but I gritted my teeth and stopped them from coming.

I wouldn't be weak.

I *couldn't* be weak.

"I'm fine," I said, taking a step back.

Pushing a lock of hair away from my face, I cleared my throat and tried not to let the whole situation become even more awkward. "Let's get moving. It's going to get dark soon."

And so we continued, not a word more between us.

IQ'HER

What little bit of food that Stasia and I had found was gone. Everyone got a small bit, but not enough to satisfy anyone's hunger. I, despite my own training, was feeling the effects of little to no food, as well. However, I was confident that I was much more able to survive no rations longer than any of these humans.

So far, nearly the entire group had gone out one time or another to look for food. Some people had brought back things they claimed were edible, then immediately spat out the food or retched after eating it.

Soon enough the people of the cities would also be hungry. The farmers were already complaining about their crops failing.

I thought back to my meeting with Rouhr before

any of this happened. We had talked about how we were going to need to rely on the food synthesizers before too long, and how they were going to be woefully inadequate for the population of the planet.

I thought about the synthesizers we had already installed and used within Glymna, Duvest, Einhiv, and Nyheim. They provided food for at least half of each city's population, but they relied on the minerals and scraps that were put into them to create the food we ate. If there was no natural food to put into the synthesizers, we would soon be eating food pellets.

They would keep people alive, if only barely, but they had absolutely no flavor and no satisfaction to them. Not to mention that the food pellets would run out eventually. I hoped my estimates were still on the mark. We had less than a year of food left for the entire planet.

The only hope we had when it came to using the synthesizers would be to finish dismantling the *Aurora* and use every available piece to create as many synthesizers as possible. That would give us another six months to a year if we remained on strict rationing.

A lot of people would end up very thin before this was all done.

"We need to come up with a plan," Roddik said, surprisingly calm. "We have no food, can't find any, and we need to figure out what we're going to do before we start starving to death."

There was silence for a few minutes. "Come on!" Roddik yelled, his usual anger returning in force.

I nearly chuckled as the prospect of Roddik being calm lasted a grand total of three minutes. Must have been a record for him while conscious.

Some ideas began flowing, and they were all terrible.

I just wanted that monster away from Stasia. She'd been under his tyranny for far too long, and I wished to see her carefree and happy.

"We could go back to Nyheim and steal a truck," one suggestion came out. The returning to Nyheim part was a good idea, not the stealing part.

"There's a couple of farms nearby," another one started. "We'll take their food."

Roddik seemed to like that one a bit. "Not bad, but what if they don't have enough?"

"Better than what we have now," that person responded.

"What if we go join one of the smaller settlements?"

Everyone turned to stare at me… and I turned to stare at Stasia. It had been she that had suggested it.

She looked at the group, then turned her attention to her brother. "There's a few new little settlements thanks to the Xathi attack, and I doubt they have a close connection to Nyheim. They most likely don't have any information about what we've done, so we can probably join up with them."

"That's not bad," Roddik said. "You're not completely useless, then." I wanted to punch him so badly. He turned to the group. "So, what do you all think about that idea? Go join one of the newer places?"

"What if they don't like us?" a woman asked.

"Yeah!" one of the bigger men said. "What if they don't want us there?"

Chaos erupted immediately.

"How do we get food?"

"Where would we stay?"

"What if they call those aliens?"

"Yeah, what if they call the aliens and they come for us? What do we do?"

For nearly an hour, the conversation degenerated into more alien bashing and questions about what to do.

Before long, the idea came up that, instead of joining one of the new settlements, they would take over one of the settlements.

"No!" Stasia yelled out. "What is wrong with you people?"

She had the patience of a saint, but this insanity could try it.

The crowd turned on her quickly. "Wrong with us?"

Roddik asked, mimicking his sister's tone. "What the hell do you mean?"

"How could you think about taking over one of the settlements?" Stasia pointed at him. "You're thinking about attacking a group of innocent people for no other reason than they *might* disagree with you."

Roddik waved her off as if what she was saying made no sense. "Whatever. Look, if they don't agree with us, then they're obviously against us and will be a problem. So, instead of letting that problem be a problem, we solve the problem from the start so they won't be a problem at all."

I shook my head to clear it, thanks to his reasoning. He was justifying an attack, and his group was believing in the idea.

"Hey! New guy. What do you think?" Roddik asked me.

I looked around. Everyone was staring at me, even Stasia.

"Well, I agree with your sister," I said, then quickly held up my hands when Roddik glared and dropped his hand to his gun. "Look, I'm just saying that if we attack innocent people, then we end up becoming the bad guys. We'll eventually have to deal with how people will think about us, even the non-alien people."

He considered my words for a moment, giving me a tiny spark of hope that he would change his mind.

Unfortunately, he unzipped and pissed all over that spark. He shook his head and laughed at me. "Figures you would be weak like her." He jutted his chin out at Stasia.

There was nothing weak in integrity or morals, but this was not the place for having that argument. I clenched my fists before I could stop myself, but quickly unclenched them.

He turned to the crowd. "Let's do this democratically, shall we? Who votes for being weak-ass cowards and asking *politely* for people to take us in?"

Stasia and I were the only ones to raise our hands.

"Okay," he laughed. "Now, who votes for taking what we deserve and creating a humans-only place to live?" Everyone else raised their hands. "See?" he said smugly, looking at us and giving us a painfully sadistic smile. "No one but you two thinks it's a good idea to be little pussies."

I opened my mouth to say something, but closed it.

"What? Nothing to say?" he asked me in a mocking tone. "You two better decide where your loyalties lie. We've got plans to make." As Roddik and his group of five trusted cronies began to plan out their next movements, I looked for Stasia.

She took herself a little ways away and began pacing. I took that opportunity to make my own way away from the group. I walked near one of the small structures, snuck in, and stole a small human comm radio I'd had my eye on.

Taking myself several hundred yards away from the campsite, I climbed up a tree. I manipulated the comm, playing with the channels until I managed to find one that was connected to a *Vengeance* broadcast frequency.

"This is *Vengeance, Rogue*, can anyone hear me?" I called through the little human comm.

"Come in *Rogue*, you are broadcasting," was the answer.

"Acknowledged. Have you received my transmissions? Awaiting orders."

A click, and Rouhr was patched through. "I've been leaving them alone on their camping trip, to lure other like-minded individuals out. But we can't let them continue with this plan. What are your suggestions, *Rogue?*"

I took a breath, and spent half a second thinking. "When the group shows up, put up minimal resistance, then evacuate. Let them settle back down, but keep them bottled up."

"Understood, *Rogue*. Be careful. Good luck."

I turned off the radio, and climbed back down the tree. There was too much at stake here, and too many variables. Roddik was out of his mind and only getting more violent and angry. I would have to find just the right moment to get Stasia out of the group and away from her brother. This group was beginning to get too far out of control.

Something needed to happen. This group needed to be stopped. I had no qualms over their hatred and dislike for my kind and the others, everyone was entitled to their opinions.

There were races and species that I didn't like.

Skrell, the Xathi were simply hated by us all, so I could feel some empathy towards someone hating another simply because of what species they were.

However, the idea of them attacking people simply because they had a different opinion about how they should live, that was wrong.

I had to get back to the campsite before anyone noticed I was gone.

I took a deep breath, shook my head in wonder, and made my way back.

I currently hated Roddik and these humans for being so stupid and giving in to that most idiotic of things, the mob mentality.

For putting my mate, even if she hadn't acknowledged it yet, in danger.

If any harm came to her, then they would have every reason to fear this alien.

STASIA

"Fuck you, Roddik!" I cried out in frustration, kicking the tree in front of me as hard as I could.

Roddik was out of earshot, so he didn't hear what I had just said. That was for the best, of course, even though I was aching to say it to his face. Oh, and not just that... I had a lot of things I wanted to say to his face. "Screw all this shit!" I continued, kicking the tree as hard as I could, over and over again.

I only stopped when pain shot up my foot and, for a moment, I thought I had broken one of my toes. I sat on the ground, cursing my luck, and gritted my teeth so damn hard I could've broken them. My brother was completely out of control, and it seemed that anything I did to help only made matters worse.

How the hell had we gone from building a peaceful

settlement to planning an invasion? Who the hell did Roddik think he was? A brigand? A new generation of highwayman? He had always liked his space pirates holomovies when he was younger, but I guess he never realized the pirates were the bad guys.

Sitting up, I leaned back against a tree and tried to calm myself. As pissed off as I was, kicking a tree while shouting curses at my brother wouldn't help my situation. No...now, more than ever, I needed to keep my cool.

Looking up, I saw that the group was still debating Roddik's plan, but they were only concerned with the details. No one but me or Iq'her seemed to bother with ethics, it seemed. If they had to resort to pillaging the countryside to get some food in their bellies, then that was exactly what they were going to do.

For a moment, I almost wished Iq'her had just called one of the strike teams and told them to show up here. At least this nightmare would come to an end. Of course, if Iq'her did that, it was almost a certainty that people would die. I didn't see anyone here surrendering peacefully, after all.

"Hold on," I muttered, still glancing at the group.

Only now that I was thinking of Iq'her did I realize he was missing. I scanned the entire clearing with a glance, and my heart sunk when I didn't see him anywhere. His bags remained next to his lean-to shelter, sure, but that didn't mean a thing.

Scared, I jumped up to my feet.

Could it be possible that Iq'her had decided to leave? Leave me?

I wouldn't be too surprised if he was already on his way back to Nyheim, ready to rejoin his team. If that was the case, then I was pretty sure that he'd show up here before the day was over, except this time he'd be bringing a team of armed aliens with him. And all because Roddik had decided he wanted to be a conqueror.

I had no choice: Roddik had to be stopped before it was too late.

Pushing myself up to my feet, I swallowed whatever hesitancy I was feeling and made my way back toward the group. A few heads turned in my direction, but no one really stopped me as I closed the distance between me and Roddik. He only noticed me when I was a couple of feet away from him.

"What the hell do you want now?" he asked, stopping whatever he was saying to face me. "Don't tell me you want to pitch the coward's way again, Stasia."

"It's not the coward's way." I clenched my fists. "You're not a murderer, Roddik, so let's put a stop to this. What do you think is going to happen if you take over a settlement? If the capital hears about it, you're going to have the aliens after you. You've heard about their strike teams, haven't you? How long do you think any of us will survive if they decide to come after us?"

"Damn, Stasia," he sighed. "I knew you were weak… I just didn't know you were this pathetic."

"You're the one who's pathetic, you little shit," I growled, taking one step toward him as my blood started to boil. I was more than ready to punch his smug face. "Why don't you stop behaving like a child, Roddik? You're a grown man, aren't you? So stop fucking around. It's time you act responsibly. These people are counting on you!"

"And that's exactly why we're going to do this," he spat back at me, a vein throbbing on his forehead. He looked angrier than I had ever seen him before, which was to be expected: Roddik wasn't used to people standing up to him. "And either get with the problem or I will—"

"You'll what?" I defied him to continue, even though I didn't want to hear his reply.

"Let's calm down!" I heard Iq'her's voice say, and I turned around to see him walking toward us. He had his holobelt on, which meant he still wanted to keep his disguise. Apparently, I had jumped the gun when I thought he had left. Whatever he was planning, it didn't involve abandoning the group.

"This is none of your fucking business!" Roddik

shouted toward Iq'her, but his words seemed to have missed his target. Iq'her just ignored my brother and, before anyone could stop him, he walked up to me and draped one arm over my shoulders.

"I'm sorry, Roddik, just trying to keep the peace," he said, and I suddenly realized he was trying to defuse the situation. In a way, that was infuriating. I almost wanted him to turn the damn holobelt off, reveal himself, and kick the shit out of Roddik. As it was, he settled on the other available option.

"Come, Stasia," he whispered, and I followed his lead.

We walked out of the circle that had formed around Roddik and made our way toward the edge of the clearing.

"Yeah, walk away, you cowards!" Roddik jeered, but Iq'her didn't allow me to reply.

He just held me tight and guided me out of the clearing, only stopping when we were by ourselves.

"Roddik isn't going to be swayed like that," Iq'her finally said, his tone so casual it almost seemed like he was talking about the weather. "I appreciate what you were trying to do, but your brother isn't going to change his mind." His arms were wrapped tightly around me now.

"Yeah, well, I had to try," I said, inhaling the strange,

musky scent of him. "If I don't stop him, that idiot is going to end up dead."

"Stasia…" He hesitated for a moment, and I could tell he wasn't sure how to continue. I wondered if he intentionally pulled me closer to him. "Why do you care so much about Roddik? I know that he is your brother, but he has so little respect for you. And yet, you care for him. You protect him. It doesn't make any sense."

"Don't you think I know that?" I replied, an unintended edge to my voice. I started to pull away now. "I know that he doesn't give a damn about me. But he's my brother… I can't just abandon him! You saw how he's acting. If I don't keep my eyes on him, he's going to end up dead."

I slumped to the ground then, all strength leaving my body. I hadn't realized how much I was leaning on Iq'her.

I felt exhausted, probably more than I had ever felt in my entire life. Ever since our parents had died, Roddik had become my number one priority, but he wasn't the same person from before. He had turned into a hateful little man, and still… I simply couldn't let go of him.

"I don't know what to do," I admitted, my voice so faint that the slightest breeze could've carried my words away. "I'm just so freaking lost. I hate him but…I promised my parents I would *always* look after him, Iq'her. I can't break that promise. I simply can't."

Then the tears came.

I tried to stop them, but this time I simply couldn't. They rolled down my cheeks effortlessly, and the moment one of them reached my lips, a violent sob shook my whole body. Iq'her went down on one knee in front of me and, looking into my eyes, pulled me into an embrace, his strong, massive arms helping to erase some of my pain.

But the sobs kept coming, the floodgates had opened and emotions were pouring from me.

"I've failed already, haven't I?" I sobbed, my heart breaking into a million little pieces. "My brother... he's lost, and there's no finding him. I've failed, Iq'her. I'm useless."

"No, you're not," he whispered into my ear. "You're the bravest woman I've ever met, Stasia. And it's not your fault your brother turned out the way he has. It's no one's fault... war does strange things to people, and there's no controlling that. And for what it's worth, I'm truly sorry. I'm sorry the Xathi came to this planet because of us, and I'm sorry you've had to endure all of this." After a short pause, he laid one hand on the nape of my neck, caressing my skin with his fingers.

"It's not your fault, either," I told him. "You're trying to help."

"I am. But the things I did...I had no right to spy on you, Stasia. Had I known that—"

"No," I cut him short. "I didn't like it at first, but now I'm glad that you put the tracker on me. Roddik... he needs to be stopped, and I can't do it alone."

"I'm right here. We'll fix this."

"I just want it all to end," I said. "And I want to go home."

"And you will. I promise you." He held me tight, and I laid my head on his chest. For a short while, neither of us said a thing. I just let him calm me down, the warmth of his body having a soothing effect on mine. For the first time in months, I felt safe. More than that, I felt that I had finally met someone that truly cared for me.

With Iq'her, I didn't feel alone anymore.

"Thank you," I breathed out, looking up into his eyes.

"For what?"

"For being here."

With that, I just let instinct guide me.

I stretched upward and brushed my lips against his. His mouth felt just right and, even if for just a fraction of a second, nothing else seemed to matter. I could feel his hands on my back. He was pulling me closer to him and I let myself go.

I didn't want to resist.

I felt his strong hands caress me and I rubbed my body against his. I was acting wantonly but I didn't care. All I cared about was kissing him.

The rest of Ankau could go to hell for all I cared.

Only when I pulled back from him did I realize what I had just done.

My emotions had taken over me, and I had surrendered myself to Iq'her.

Thing is… I would gladly do it again.

"I'm going to protect you," he said, holding my chin up with two fingers. "I'm going to keep you safe, Stasia, and that's a promise."

IQ'HER

I escorted Stasia back to the campsite. Most of the humans were sitting around the campfire, talking. I wasn't able to hear what they were talking about, not from where we were.

After a moment's hesitation, I flicked the bug still in my pocket to tracking only. It was unlikely that we'd pick up any new information from Roddik tonight, and I'd violated Stasia's trust enough on this mission.

Whoever had been assigned to monitor this channel didn't need to hear any more of her personal business.

"Are you going to be okay?" I asked her quietly as I brought her over to her lean-to. It wasn't badly built, but the tree she had attached it to looked as if it was dying. Things were progressing far too fast in regard to the death of the vegetation. It wasn't natural. It wasn't safe.

She shook her head. "No, but I'll find some way through it. I always do." She was still upset and hurt by Roddik, I could see it in her eyes and hear it in her voice.

She was on the verge of being broken.

The kiss that we had shared a few minutes ago was still echoing inside me. The sensations that I felt in my head and in my heart the moment our lips touched were so intense, it was as if my entire life had been building to that moment. I knew, at that very instant, that I wanted to make this woman my lifemate. There was nothing else in existence that I wanted more than to spend my life with her and make her smile.

Knowing that her brother treated her the way he did, I wanted to put him into a coma, then take his comatose body and bury the body parts in so many different places that no deity in the history of deities could ever find them all.

She had to be my mate.

There was no other reason my logic, my control, would totally abandon me.

Nothing else mattered but her.

I helped her into her lean-to and sat down outside the 'entrance' to it. "Is there anything I can do?" I asked.

She shook her head. "No. He's my brother. I have to

figure it out. I don't want you getting hurt because of me."

"I won't get hurt. I was trained for things like this," I said softly.

She looked up at me, her eyes still red from having cried so much. "You've been trained to take care of an emotional sister while her jackass brother tries to overrun a human settlement just because they *might* be friendly towards other races?"

"Well," I said with an exaggerated smirk, "if you really must know, it was covered in the second week of training. I scored the highest marks."

Despite herself, she laughed. It was nice to see her happy, even if it was only for a short moment. Her laughter, no matter what anyone could ever tell me, was the most beautiful sound I had ever heard.

I arched my eyebrows several times and smiled a goofy smile meant just for her. She snorted as she tried to hold back her laughter. After a few short moments, she stopped laughing. "Thank you for making me feel a little better," she said.

"It was my honor and pleasure, m'lady," I said with a mock bow.

She smiled again, but this smile looked forced and a bit sad. "I'm tired. Will I see you in the morning?"

"Without a doubt."

"Okay." She nodded slowly. "Good night, Ilkay," she said, using the human name I had chosen.

"Good night, Stasia," I replied, not moving.

"You're not going anywhere?"

I looked at her. Her lithe figure called me. Her beautiful face beckoned me.

"I want to make sure you're alright."

She took two steps back to me.

"You're my protector?" she asked.

I nodded.

"You want to take care of me?"

"Always."

"Will you comfort me?"

"I will."

She took two more steps. Now she was less than a foot from me. I could smell the fragrance of her hair.

I could see the swell of her breasts. Her chest heaved upwards with each breath she took.

When she saw me looking at her, she gave a short gasp.

"Will you let me comfort you?"

I did not answer. Instead, I brought my arms around her and pulled her close. She brought her mouth to mine.

I felt her delicate little mouth as her tongue parted my lips. My tongue darted out and she was ready.

I felt her breath on me. My skin was on fire. I felt

her hands on my throat, as they felt the muscles on my chest. She moaned into my mouth and I picked her up.

Stasia wrapped her legs around me as my hands caressed her plump bottom. I squeezed her lush hips and she gasped.

I bit her neck and she tried as hard as she could to remain silent.

We had to be quiet. The sounds of our passion could not penetrate the forest and bring others to our location.

But I had to have her. I couldn't wait. I needed to give her the pleasure that she had given me with her presence.

I set Stasia down.

"Iq'her…" she began, but I shushed her. Instead, I turned her around.

She hesitated briefly before letting me move her body until she was nestled against me, her back pressed into my chest.

With gentle strokes, I ran my hands over her breasts.

"Squeeze them, Iq'her," she moaned softly. "Harder."

I complied. My hands moved of their own accord as I took each mound of flesh in my hands and rubbed them through her shirt. She squirmed and hissed in pleasure and I managed to move my hands under her shirt, where I was able to pay her breasts closer attention.

My cock, always hard in her presence, threatened to burst through my pants.

It was throbbing. Blood pounded in my ears and I tried desperately to remember my surroundings. We were in hostile territory and I needed to stay alert.

But then Stasia backed up, impossibly closer, and rubbed herself against my thickened and engorged cock.

"Do you like that?" she asked in a whisper. "Is this better than saying goodnight?"

I growled and pushed it harder against her. She cooed and began to jerk herself against it, as if she was trying to impale herself with her pants still on.

We did not have time to couple, but I knew what to do for her.

Lifting her against me, I backed us away from her lean-to, further into the woods, where we'd be safe from prying eyes. I carefully undid the buttons to her pants and let them fall. I eased down her underclothes and brought them to her ankles.

I put one hand over her mouth.

"You must be silent," I whispered in her ear. "No one must hear."

She nodded as my other hand traveled from her breasts, down to her stomach, and finally came to a rest over her naked mound.

She gave a soft 'ooh' as my fingers traversed over her slit.

She was wet. Her juices were already leaking from her and travelling down her legs. She began to kick her legs until her pants were off and her legs could separate unencumbered.

And that's when I used my index finger to travel from the top of her slit down.

"Fuck, Iq'her," she hissed from behind my hand. "Your finger feels so good."

I began to run my finger over her slick folds over and over. Human female physiology was something that I had read about after meeting Stasia in the restaurant and it took me only a few seconds to find what she referred to as…

"My clit. Oh god. Oh god," she moaned.

I placed two fingers over the hood and began to move them in a circular motion, bending my knees slightly to lift her from the ground, supporting her slight weight on my thighs.

Her head lolled back onto my chest as she felt herself suspended in midair as explosions of pleasure hit her body. I could feel her muscles spasm and buck as my fingers worked on her. Stasia's head rolled to the side as she attempted to get words out.

"Quiet," I whispered to her, reminding her of her part of this bargain.

And I plunged my fingers in deep into her tight heat.

If Stasia could have shrieked, every living creature in the area would know what was going on. But instead, she kicked her feet against my legs as she lost control of her limbs.

I kept thrusting my fingers into her, going deeper each time. Once completely inside of her, I made a come-hither motion with my fingers against her walls, and once again Stasia exploded.

Bringing pleasure to my mate was perhaps one of the most satisfying endeavors in the universe.

There she was, helpless in my arms as I kept her suspended in midair. Her legs thrashed. Her head rolled from side to side. Her breathing was short and ragged as orgasm after orgasm consumed her.

"So good…" she moaned.

"This is but a taste," I informed her, my breath hot on her ear. "Speaking of such things…"

I lifted her higher, turning her until her sweet pussy was in front of my face and she clasped my shoulders with desperate fingers.

"Can you be quiet without my help?" I demanded.

"I don't know, I don't know…" she started.

But it was too late for caution. I drove into her dripping folds with my tongue, lapping her nectar until she wrapped her legs around my shoulders, her hands fisting on my scalp.

Two licks. And then three more and she collapsed onto me, shuddering in bliss.

I stood there for a long moment, breathing deeply of her scent.

My mate.

Happy and relaxed.

Because of me.

If I'd thought I would do anything for her before, that was nothing to the feeling of possession that washed through me now.

I should take her from this cursed forest, away from her idiot brother.

Lock her in the new home, drive her to a screaming mess in my arms, over and over.

And she'd never trust me again.

I'd promised to try to bring this disaster to a peaceful conclusion.

Let her brother have every chance.

And so, I would.

For her.

Gently holding her as her shaky knees re-accustomed themselves, I helped her put her pants back on.

"Well, these panties are ruined," she said with a smile.

With her leaning on my arm, we started back towards her lean-to then, against my better judgement, shared a furtive kiss that was laced with desire.

"Good night, Stasia." I bid her. "Stay safe. I'll be near."

I watched as she nestled down in the scant bedding, obviously uncomfortable.

After this, never again, I swore as I made my way over to the campfire, curious as to what was being said. Roddik sounded uncharacteristically calm, and that worried me.

"My brother and his family were killed when those things arrived. I've never been able to forgive them like my sister has," I heard one of the men saying as I took a seat along the outer circle of people.

Another one nodded. "Same here. My wife forgave the bastards and even started working with them when we lived back in Duvest. I moved everyone to Nyheim after the bugs were killed, thinking the rest of the aliens would leave, but they didn't."

"What happened to your wife, Dunk?" one of Roddik's closest people asked.

"*Ex*-wife," the one called Dunk said. "She said that my refusal to give them the benefit of the doubt wasn't something she wanted to be a part of." His voice was filled with love and forgiveness when he mentioned her, but as soon as he mentioned us in any way, the hatred in his voice dripped.

"Look," one of the women cut in. "I can sort of forgive them for crashing here, it was an accident. But why are they still here? Why are they trying to run our lives? Who put them in charge?"

This got several nods after the initial groan of her opening.

In a way, I understood her point. Who did put us in charge, exactly? It just seemed as though, in our attempt to make up for the damage we had caused, we just took over the running of things.

While Vidia was Nyheim's unofficial mayor and ran the city, her relationship with him meant that Rouhr had free rein to do what he felt was necessary to get things done in the best way.

Of course, the 'best' way seemed to be *our* way, so...

"How can you forgive them for even coming here?" Roddik demanded of the woman. His voice was calm, however, so she merely took it as a simple question, not as the hate-filled challenge that I knew it was.

"Well, they were in a fight with the Xathi, the rift opened up and they were pulled through. It wasn't their fault that they got caught in our gravity and crashed down," she explained.

"Wasn't it?" Roddik countered. "What if they opened the rift themselves?"

"Why would they do that?" someone asked.

Roddik shrugged. "To send the Xathi away. What if they were sending the Xathi somewhere and just go sucked in behind them?"

"Wait," Dunk said. "Are you trying to say that they sent the Xathi here…on purpose?"

Roddik nodded. "Think about it. They dropped the Xathi on top of us, then those things attacked and started killing us. But, if you think about it, after the Xathi's initial frenzy, they had slowed down. They were communicating with some of us."

"What about the people that they were transforming, though?" someone asked.

"What if that was our 'heroes' in order to make a new enemy? Keep themselves *needed* by us." Roddik answered. "Then they had to kill them all off when those other ones showed up, those tall blue things. Now, as our 'heroes,' they run the joint."

It was nothing like that. We certainly didn't bring the Xathi here on purpose, and we most assuredly weren't the ones that were creating the hybrids.

"So, then why? Just to take our food?" the woman Roddik had questioned asked.

He nodded. "Think it through. We haven't had an issue with the food in the generations we've been on this planet. Now, the plants are suddenly dying and they call for a rationing system. Are they really sending those shipments to the other settlements or keeping it for themselves?"

"Why would they do that? They're stuck on this planet just like we are. We don't even have a shuttle that can make it out of the atmosphere anymore," another one of the women countered. "They don't have a way off the planet."

"But if they can starve most of us to death, then miraculously *save* us… we'll fall to our knees and worship our saviors," Roddik said acidly. "Just look at what they've done in Nyheim. They took over office buildings and labs. Their soldiers are buying up the homes and are spending money like it was nothing. You have another explanation?"

That started a small discussion. Not everyone followed Roddik's way of thinking, but the numbers seemed to be growing. I saw three people that I knew weren't completely on Roddik's side as of this morning, suddenly agreeing with everything he said.

"They're taking our food, our supplies, our women, and act like they're in charge," one of Roddik's people took over the conversation, allowing Roddik to sit back with a look of pride on his face. It was almost as if he had won this round against us, and I was inclined to agree.

He had more people believing in his words, believing his interpretation of what had happened.

"That's why we need to get away from them. We need to rebuild our homes and rebuild our lives *without* their influence. I'm not trying to be racist... or species-ist... but we were living pretty well before they brought their war to us," Roddik's man was saying. "We need to show, not only those alien bastards, but other humans as well, that *we* are the ones that run our lives. *We* decide what happens to us, not *them*. Agreed?"

More and more nods in agreement.

Roddik leaned forward, his hand on the shoulder of his speaker. "Then we need to establish ourselves. We need to put ourselves in position to be self-sustaining, not needing the help of those fucking things." His voice was eerily calm, and it seemed to suck in his listeners. "We take over a settlement. *We* run it, make it grow, and show that it can and will survive without them. More people will come, and we'll let them in. This is *our* home. Let's make sure it stays that way."

I could almost understand their feelings, almost.

Their desire and willingness to violently take over one of their own towns sort of ruined the empathy I felt for them.

"Everyone get some sleep, we leave first thing in the morning," Roddik said.

As camp broke up and everyone headed to wherever they were going to sleep, Roddik glared at me, then softened his stare.

"Thank you for caring for my sister," he said to me. The care in his voice sounded sincere, genuine. Damn, he was good at this.

"Not a problem," I said. "Glad I could help."

"Hmm." He looked at me for a few more moments, then turned away from me.

Skrell.

He was learning to be convincing. To keep his temper in check.

But I could still see the madness in his eyes.

And Stasia would be in the middle of whatever plan he devised, trying to keep him safe, even against his own darker instincts.

Double skrell.

STASIA

W e set out at first light.
Everyone seemed happy to leave the clearing behind, even if that meant the shelters we had painfully, sloppily built were now going to be abandoned. Somehow, Roddik had managed to play the situation to his advantage.

The group's mood had been growing somber, the dream of building a settlement vanished as quickly as our food reserves...and yet, Roddik had managed to bring the group together once more, promising them a brighter future for the second time.

And just like the idiots they were, they swallowed it hook, line, and sinker.

"Are we really gonna go forward with this?" I asked Iq'her. We were walking together, occupying the rear of the line made by the group. The trail we used was a small one, and no more than two people could walk side by side at any given moment. But we were walking close enough that our hands brushed repeatedly as we were walking.

"For the time being, yes. Let's just play along," he responded, his voice resolute. Even though I had no idea what he was thinking, I had no other option but to trust him. "I have a plan, Stasia."

"Care to share?"

"Not right now," he smiled, using his hatchet to cut down a few branches that were in my way. "I want to keep it under wraps. But don't worry. I won't let anything crazy happen."

"I hope you're right," I sighed. 'Crazy' was one of Roddik's specialties, after all. "Where are we going, anyway?"

"I'm not sure," Iq'her admitted. "I talked to your brother before we set out, but he didn't want to share our destination. Judging by the direction we're going in, though, I think I have an idea. There's a small settlement between Nyheim and Fraga, one that was built just a few years ago, and it's no more than a few hours away from where we are right now. If I had to guess, that's your brother's target."

"How do you know all that?" I asked him. I was surprised that he seemed to know more about the human settlements surrounding Nyheim than most people.

"I've been working very closely with General Rouhr since we settled in Nyheim," he answered. "I organized some of the food drops in the surrounding settlements, and I ended up memorizing some of the maps."

"Showoff." I startled myself when I realized I was laughing. I couldn't remember the last time I had laughed, and yet here I was... chuckling over some stupid joke I had made. Somehow, Iq'her's presence made me feel like a normal woman. Maybe, after all this was over, I could still see him again...

It was hard to admit, but I liked the way he made me feel. Even when he wasn't touching me, I could still feel his touch, his hands that held me, keeping me safe.

Protecting me.

"QUIET NOW!" Roddik hissed from the front, raising one closed fist. "We're just a few minutes away from the nearest settlement. The scouts I've sent told me there are five alien guards on the perimeter, so we have to be careful. We're going to need the element of surprise."

It was odd, but Roddik was slowly starting to grow into his role as a leader. I never really thought it would happen, but he was starting to prove me wrong.

Of course, that wasn't exactly a good thing... Roddik was becoming a true leader, yes, but his leadership was a cruel one.

The whole group followed Roddik to the edge of the forest, and then he ordered us to scatter and wait for his signal. I did as I was told, Iq'her never leaving my side. I had a hunting knife in my belt, but I wasn't exactly sure what I was going to do with it. I didn't want to attack innocent people and, even if I wanted to, my knife would be useless against a rifle.

Lying down on the round, my belly pressed against the grass, I looked at the small settlement in front of us.

Just like Roddik had said, there were five alien guards at the edge of town. They all had guns, but they didn't seem particularly alert. That didn't surprise me — the Xathi had been defeated, and there was no major threat lurking in the shadows.

Besides, the small settlement was exactly that: a small cluster of squat buildings and a tiny avenue that ran the length of the town. I wasn't entirely sure, but if I had to guess, I would've said there couldn't be more than fifty people living there.

It made sense for Roddik to have chosen such a target. Our numbers weren't that great, so he had to make sure the settlement he chose wouldn't put up a fight. If the human civilians didn't fight back, then we'd only have to deal with five alien guards. They could be dangerous, yes, but the numbers were on our side.

"I don't like this," I whispered at Iq'her, watching as some of the men in the group started grabbing their guns. Apparently, some had brought more than just axes and hunting knives from the city.

"It's going to be fine," Iq'her tried to calm me, but my heart was already racing at a hundred miles an hour. I was supposed to be waiting tables, not fighting a goddamn war!

"NOW!" Roddik screamed all of a sudden, and everyone jumped to their feet. Roddik's right hand man, a tall bald-headed guy, led the charge. He started shooting at the guards with the old rifle he was carrying, all the while screaming like a complete maniac.

The guards reacted fast, running for cover the moment the first shot was fired. They huddled together behind a small wall that ran across the length of one of the houses, and only when they were safe did they start shooting back.

While some of the men started advancing toward the settlement, firing a shot with each step they took, I fell behind and hid behind a line of trees. No way was I going to be a part of this madness.

"Stay here," Iq'her told me, and then he joined the rest of the men. There was a gun in his hands, one that I assumed had been given to him by Roddik or one of the others. He fired it multiple times, but he never really seemed to hit the mark.

Suffice to say, that was odd.

When the guards finally left the wall they were hiding behind, they started laying suppressive fire as they made their retreat. I quickly realized they were shooting exactly like Iq'her.

They looked fierce and determined, but their marksmanship was a complete mess. I didn't know much about the aliens, but I was under the impression that all of them were veteran soldiers... and, judging from how they fought against the Xathi, they were damn good at their jobs.

And now here they were, purposefully acting like rookies. All just so they wouldn't decimate Roddik's group. In the back of my mind, I knew that most aliens weren't bad guys, but I had never realized just how patient they were with the humans they had to live with.

"They're falling back!" I heard Roddik shout as the aliens turned a corner and disappeared behind a row of houses. That seemed to make Roddik's rebels even bolder than before, and they started rushing toward the settlement without any caution at all. It didn't take a genius to realize that what they were doing was stupid —if the aliens decided to turn back, Roddik and his men would be caught in the open...and, without cover, they'd be easy pickings.

In the end, the aliens' mercy was the only thing keeping my brother alive.

"WE FUCKING DID IT!" Roddik shrieked, firing a few shots into the air. A few others joined him, shouting victory like madmen. It seemed that the concept of rationing was completely foreign to them, even when it came to ammunition.

Thankfully, the alien guards seemed to have bolted, or else we'd be pretty screwed.

"What the hell just happened?" I asked Iq'her as I joined him near the edge of the settlement. "Those guards... they could've put up a fight."

"I know," Iq'her said, and then he winked at me.

All part of his plan.

IQ'HER

"Find everyone!" Roddik ordered us. "Find every single one of them and get them out here. If they don't want to give us their valuables and supplies, then we'll just take them!"

Too many people cheered.

I stepped up. "Do we really want to force the human residents of this town?"

"You got a better idea, Ilkay?" he asked sourly.

"Well, maybe." I shrugged. "What if we talk to them and get them to join us?"

"Hmm?"

"Think about it," I held up one finger, "One, you've only got twenty-some people part of this right now. Two," I held up a second finger. "We know there are others that feel the same way as us."

I held up a third finger, "Three, what if some people here, or even all of them, feel the same as you? What if they aren't alien lovers? What if they were just using those aliens that just ran away? We convince them to join the cause and you've got a bigger following."

"You know what, Ilkay? You're not as dumb as you look," he said with a smile. "That's actually a brilliant idea." He turned to the others, and this time, without the anger and hatred, yelled out, "Find everyone, but be nice to our new friends. We don't want any confusion about what we're here for."

Oh, the charm he suddenly put on was disturbing. As the first… villagers… were brought out, Roddik put on a smile and talked to them calmly.

"My friends, I am so, so sorry for the confusion and excitement that we've caused. We certainly didn't mean to cause any problems for you fine people," he said to the few that were already there. He smiled at the 'newcomers' that were brought to the center of this tiny little place, many of them families.

"Again," he said loudly to make sure everyone heard him, "I sincerely apologize for the commotion that we've created. We did not mean to disturb you or scare you. We are actually here to help you."

"What do you mean, 'help' us?" an elderly man asked as a small child of three or four hid behind his leg.

"Well, sir." Roddik was respectful and kind. I was

worried. "We're here to push the alien incursion away. We've heard reports…"

"What incursion?" the old man interrupted. "Those men you ran off were helping us get established."

Roddik smiled at the interruption. "Yes, sir. I'm sure that they were. I'm not doubting that," he said, making sure to be polite and respectful in his tone. "But, as I'm sure you've noticed, the plants that we rely on are dying and we're running out of food."

"Yeah. They said it was because of some big creature that was controlling the plants," the elderly one said.

"Sir, may I ask your name?"

"Name's Porter. Yours?"

"Well, Porter, my name is Roddik. I come from Nyheim where the aliens were trying to help us repair and rebuild… but then the dome of vines came over our city. They were responsible for the dome," he lied. "If anyone other than one of their own tried to find a way out, they killed them."

The last few words, a blatant lie, were met with gasps. Roddik quickly explained how the vines erupted from the ground and formed the dome, then how a human had found a way to bring the dome down.

"I don't believe that they would hurt us," a young one that looked to be a teenager said. "These guys were so nice to us and helped us with everything."

Roddik didn't even flinch. "They were the same way

back home," he lied again. "They were so nice and helpful. Then, a friend of mine said that he'd found a way out of the dome and went to tell the alien leader. My friend's body was found in an alley the next day. The aliens said he must have been attacked and killed by criminals." He even put pain and a little bit of shake into his voice to sell his story.

He was getting better at this.

I could see that he was gaining followers already.

This wasn't what I had in mind. I didn't want him to *actually* become more influential and more powerful, I just didn't want people to get hurt if they resisted.

I was sick to my stomach as more and more people started asking him questions, buying into his fabrications. I couldn't stand it any longer.

I left to find Stasia. I realized my thoughts always went to her, protecting her. I cared about the general good, but I wanted her safe above anything else.

After looking into a few of the small dwellings, I found her in the village's general store, if you could call it that. It was a tiny little building filled with some food and general supplies, but it didn't look big enough to support this tiny village.

I found her in one of the back corners, talking to about eight or nine people, trying to calm them down. "I promise you, we're not here to hurt you," I heard her say. The inflection in her voice let me know that she had already said it several times and was just doing it again with the mentality that repetition would make it true.

"We heard gunshots outside," a portly lady said as she stood protectively in front of a pregnant woman, two children, and some young ones that looked like teenagers.

"I know, and I apologize for that. My brother tends to be a bit overzealous sometimes," she explained. She went on to explain what the group was there for, but without the lies that Roddik was spinning.

The woman, I guessed that she was the shop owner based on the apron that she wore that had a logo stitched into it that matched the logo on the window, continued to glare at Stasia, and at me, but nodded.

Stasia turned her head and seemed relieved to see me.

She whispered something to the woman and headed over towards me. "I hope I won't be made out to be a liar," she whispered to me.

"No, I don't think you will," I whispered back. "Your brother is doing a fantastic job of being charming and polite right now."

She looked at me as though something were growing out of my head. "My brother?"

I nodded.

"My brother?" she asked again. "The one that treats

me like shit, talks bad about you and your crew, and essentially wants to kill anything and everything not human? The one that has reinvented the word 'asshole'?"

I had to chuckle a bit at the last question, but I nodded. "He's super charming, polite, and respectful. He's also lying through his teeth," I added as Stasia continued to look at me as though I had a second head or something.

When I mentioned that he was lying, Stasia nodded in understanding. "Oh, that's why he's being nice. It's not working, is it?"

"I'm afraid it is," I answered as I reached out for her. She allowed me to lead her to the window and I pointed at the crowd of people surrounding him. It wasn't just members of the original group, there were several villagers there as well, still talking to him.

What made me tense up was the sight of three of them bringing out food and drinks. "Skrell."

Stasia elbowed me. "Careful."

Right. "Shit."

She looked up at me, grinning slightly. "That I can agree with."

She stepped away from the window and headed back to the people in the back. "Now, my brother, or whoever he decides to send in here, is going to tell you that we're here to save you, and eventually the planet."

"You're not?" the pregnant lady asked.

"Sort of," Stasia answered. "The plants are dying, and food is running out, so we're trying to find a way to stop that. But he's going to tell you that it's the fault of those men that fell from space, that they're the reason all of this is happening."

"Is it?" the pregnant one asked as she stood up.

Stasia looked back at me, a look of loss and regret on her face. "I… I don't know," she finally said. I felt a pang in my stomach when she said it. Her statement hurt, just a little. I knew we weren't responsible… were we?

Would the Puppet Master have awoken, or whatever it did, if we had never arrived on the planet and caused as much damage as we had with our crash landings and then the battles that happened afterwards?

Was Roddik right? Were we the reason things had gotten bad and things were now getting even worse?

I was staggered by the thought.

We'd been so busy trying to keep order, keep everyone fed, I'd never truly wondered.

Was Stasia right in her disbelief and confusion about what happened and who was responsible?

My mind circled, until I didn't hear any of what they spoke about in the corner after that. Eventually, Stasia led the people out and I followed. She spoke with Roddik, and he was surprisingly kind to her. He smiled at her, gave her a hug, and nodded at whatever she said.

I followed Stasia as she started talking to people, finding out how the village was arranged, who had been in charge, and started putting together a plan to house and feed the newcomers along with the original inhabitants. With Roddik's endorsement of her, they listened to what she had to say.

I watched her as she bloomed in her role. She was a natural leader, good at what she did.

And I was left to wonder, finally, if somewhere in Roddik's hateful words was a kernel of truth.

And if so, how could I allow myself to touch her ever again?

STASIA

"Careful now," I said, holding up one of the planks as the man beside me hammered a nail into it. Some of the houses had been damaged during the fight, and I had decided to replace any shattered windows with rough wooden planks Iq'her had carved out at my request.

Not many people were happy about it, but I figured that at least the planks would stop the houses from getting cold during the night. It was only a temporary solution, anyway… or so I hoped.

"Here, miss," Alena, the pregnant woman I had met when we arrived, said as she handed me a glass of cold water.

I took it from her hands with a smile, enjoying the taste of fresh water as it touched my lips.

"I'm not a 'miss'," I told her gently. "It's just Stasia."

"Stasia," she repeated hesitantly, still unsure on how to deal with the group of newcomers. I didn't blame her. Even though my brother had fed his lies to the settlement population, a lot of people still didn't know what to make of their supposed saviors.

I felt terrible about being a part of Roddik's schemes, but I didn't have a choice. I had to play along...especially because Iq'her had been the one suggesting it. I just hoped that whatever the hell his plan was, it would work. And soon.

"I still can't believe the aliens were here to hurt us," the young woman continued, nervously shifting her weight from one foot to the other. "I mean… they were so nice. They even brought food a few days ago, right when the plants started dying around here."

"Well, these are strange times." My heart tightened into a little fist. I couldn't say much more than that — playing along was one thing, but I wouldn't help with the spreading of lies.

"You're too trusting, Alena," the man that was helping me grumbled. Judging by the ring on his finger, I guessed he was her husband. "We never needed anybody's help before. Things were going just fine before they got here."

"But it's not their fault," Alena protested.

Her husband just shrugged.

"Then who's fault is it?" he asked. "It sure as hell ain't ours."

"Damn right it isn't,'" a voice chirped from outside the house, and I saw through the gaps in the window who that voice belonged to: my brother. Grinning, he leaned against the doorway of the small house, arms folded over his chest. "I see you haven't let the aliens' propaganda fool you, my friend," he continued, offering his hand to the man. "The name's Roddik."

"I'm Uther. This is my wife, Alena."

"Nice to meet you." Roddik smiled, his words so easy and gentle that I almost didn't recognize him. How could someone so filled with hatred turn the charm up like this? "I see you have a little one on the way. Together, I'll make sure we'll build a safe future for the coming generations."

Shaking my head, I threw the nails I had been holding on top of the table and walked out of the house. No way in hell would I stay there and listen to Roddik spit his hateful lies. It was baffling the way people trusted him. He wasn't even doing anything to help repair the damages we had caused during the 'gunfight' against the aliens. Aside from walking around and trying to drum up support, the only thing he told his goons to do was to make a complete inventory of the settlement's food reserves.

I walked toward the small open square, the place

where most of Roddik's men had gathered. They had improvised a long wooden table out of some planks and tree logs, and they had hauled out all the food inside the houses and laid it there. Although I hadn't agreed to this course of action, at least I saw that some of them had followed my earlier suggestion and were now using a datapad to note how much food we had. The settlement had been struggling before we got here, and now with more mouths to feed...the days ahead would be complicated ones, I knew that.

Grabbing my bag and blanket from where I had stashed them, I paused as I tried to decide where I would stay for the night. All the men in Roddik's group had decided they'd bunk up with the families living in the settlement, but I wouldn't impose myself like that. I'd rather spend another night outside than to force my way into someone's home.

I was already at the edge of the settlement when I heard a tired voice call after me. "Stasia, isn't it?" I turned on my heels to see an elderly woman standing in the middle of the street, a long, polished limb serving as her cane. Her wrinkles cut deeply across her face, and her advanced age made her body look frail. Still, her smile was a warm one.

"That's right," I replied as politely as I could. "Can I help you?"

"I was just wondering about where you're going

with that," she asked me, jutting her chin out to point at the bag in my hand. "Don't tell me you're planning on sleeping outside, young lady."

"Well, I didn't want to cause any trouble, so I—"

"Nonsense," she cut me short, hitting the stone floor twice with her cane. She waved me over and, not knowing what else to say, I started walking toward the old woman. "No way am I going to allow that. All these men are staying indoors, so why would a pretty woman like you have to sleep in the forest? Not on my watch, miss."

"I really don't…" I started to say, but I trailed off the moment she shot me a steely glance. She might be an old woman, but she was a fiery one, all the same. "Thank you so much."

"Don't worry about that," she continued, leading the way toward her house. It was nothing but a small two-bedroom building on the edge of the settlement, but it had a certain quaintness to it. Small vases with flowers, most of them already withered, lined the cobbled path to the entrance, and there even a small garden out front. "You can call me Evna. It's just me, anyway, so I'll appreciate the company. My husband built this house with his bare hands, but those damn bugs made sure he would never build anything again."

"I'm sorry to hear that, Evna," I whispered. It seemed

that even out here, away from the largest cities, there was no escaping the heartache caused by the war.

"Well, that's life, isn't it?" She shrugged, pushing the door open and stepping inside the house. It was a small place, a small kitchen that doubled as a living room, but she kept everything spotless. "Care for some tea?" she asked, but didn't wait for my reply — she pressed the display on the kettle right away, turning it on, and then invited me to take a seat.

"It's not much, but that's what I got," she said when the tea was ready, steam rising up from the cups she had laid on the table. Between the cups was a small plate with thin slices of stale bread.

"No, this is perfect." My stomach grumbled at the sight of the bread. I couldn't remember the last time I had eaten, and the first bite I took of the bread was absolutely amazing.

For the next hour, I almost forgot about how much of a mess my life was. I was a woman sharing tea and bread with a kind old lady, not a criminal on the run. She asked me about life in the city, and I asked her about life in the settlement. Just two women making conversation.

When she finally showed me to my room, I was starting to feel like my old self. A small room with a bed, a dresser, and a shallow basin with water. So little, but so much more than I'd expected.

It seemed that there was nothing quite like the kindness of an old woman to make me feel whole again.

I was about to drift off to sleep when I heard someone knocking on the wall by my window.

I swung my legs off the bed immediately, anxiety making my heart beat faster, but then I heard Iq'her's voice.

"Stasia?" he asked, rapping his knuckles against the frame again.

"Come in."

"I just wanted to check up on you. It's been a long day." He paused, then swung easily into the room.

"I know," I sighed, moving to the side as Iq'her sat next to me. "It's been crazy, especially with my brother spouting off. I just can't take any more of this, Iq'her."

"Just hang in there," he whispered gently, then he reached for me and laid his hand on top of mine. A shiver ran up my spine as I felt the touch of his warm skin, and a warm but pleasant heat took over my body. "It'll be over before you know it."

"I hope so."

"But I don't have a choice," he continued, hesitating slightly. "Your brother and most of the group… they'll have to be detained. We can't let them go free after all they've done."

"I… I understand," I breathed out. "Roddik needs to be stopped."

"He will be. I've kept in touch with Nyheim, and it won't take long before they send one of the strike teams. Just be patient. This nightmare will be over soon enough."

"I know," I whispered, trusting Iq'her to deliver on his promises. We had started off on the wrong foot, but the more I got to know him, the more I trusted him. He was exactly the kind of man the people on this planet needed by their side, and I felt lucky to have him as my protector. And I wanted him. "Thank you, Iq'her. For everything."

"You never have to thank me." The way his eyes looked into mine made me feel like time stood still and like nothing was wrong in the world.

"You could've just ordered a strike on the group... but you didn't. You waited, you gave everyone a chance. And for that, I do have to thank you."

"No, you don't," he smiled. "In a way, I didn't do it for the group. I did it because of you, Stasia. I couldn't abandon you."

"I'm glad you didn't," I said, my heart beating just a little faster. I brushed my thumb against the palm of his hand, aching to feel more of him, and our eyes locked in that exact moment.

Time stopped, and then I just let my heart take over.

Leaning in, I closed my eyes and brushed my lips against his. He returned my kiss eagerly, his tongue parting my lips immediately, and he pressed his whole body against mine.

Slowly, as if worshiping every inch of newly exposed skin, he pulled off my clothing, raining soft kisses behind the fabric as it fell into a pile on the floor, until I was entirely naked before him.

"Wait," I breathed out, one hand on his chest. He pulled back from me and I took the chance to drop my hand to his belt. I had seen him do it once before, in the dying forest. I was sure I remembered how...

There.

Sliding the hidden plate open, I pressed down and, just like that, his human appearance faded right before my eyes.

"I want to see you," I continued, taking in every detail of him. Before, at the lean-to, he'd pleasured me, but now I wanted to witness him in all his glory.

His body was strong and muscular, the clothes outlining his strong arms and shoulders, and his dark skin seemed so alluring that I could barely think straight. Laying one hand on his forearm, I traced the green threads of biocircuitry that crawled up to his shoulders, holding my breath as I did it.

"This is me," he said, his voice soft but strong. "The *real* me."

"I like it." I closed the distance between both our bodies, my mouth crashing against his once more.

Allowing instinct to take the steering wheel, I jumped to his lap, my knees on either side of his thighs. Throwing my arms over his shoulders, I straddled him, moaning softly as I felt the hardness between his legs straining against the fabric of his pants.

"You're perfect, Stasia," he groaned, both his hands running down the sides of my body to cup my ass. He pulled me tightly against him, my breasts mashed against his chest, and we surrendered to our frenzied kiss as if nothing else in the world mattered.

The loud snoring coming from the adjoining bedroom broke the spell.

"Perfect timing," I chuckled, slowly licking my lips at Iq'her.

"We're going to have to be very quiet." he said seriously, only the trace of a smile lifting his lips. "Again."

"I know," I nodded, licking my lips. "I kinda liked it, actually."

He groaned softly. "The things you do to me, Stasia. I need to be inside you, mate."

Mate?

I turned the strange word over in my mind. I...liked it.

More than that.

"I need you, too," I breathed softly against his neck. "But first...."

I pushed him back against the mattress, hard kisses of desire and lust distracting him as he lay back.

Shifting slightly, frantically moving the fabric out of the way, I kissed my way down his chest.

I needed this alien god. I wanted every inch of him inside me. I didn't want anything less than to please him and then surrender my body to him.

But first, I wanted to repay him for earlier in the forest.

Iq'her shuddered as I brought my hands to his crotch, rubbing him through the straining fabric.

He was hard. Rock solid.

"Is this for me?" I asked quietly, looking up at him with an innocent smile. He growled, then in one quick movement, pushed the offending pants down.

I forced myself to look away, remove the boots, and pull the pants all the way down before looking back.

He lay back, supported by his elbows, black eyes fixed on my every move.

Patient.

Hungry.

Ready to devour me.

And I was ready to be consumed.

I knelt over him, then ran my hand over his thick, scaled, and rigid cock. At my first touch, he shuddered, a growl starting deep in his chest.

I lay the finger of my other hand over his lips. "Quiet, remember?"

His eyes narrowed, and I smiled and began to stroke his cock faster.

The tight band of muscle leading from his stomach to his cock twitched. With my two hands, I could bring a warrior such as him under my power. This was true power. Sure, he could destroy things. But only I could subdue him.

And then I brought my mouth to his cock. I licked the tip.

"Stasia," he growled.

I licked quickly again. He made a deep rumbling noise.

Before I could do anything further, he grabbed my hips, pulling me back over his lap, straddling his hardness.

I caught myself on his shoulders as he ground my slick core against his throbbing cock, back and forth, never actually entering my heat, just teasing at my clit with every bump and thrust as I slid against him, shuddering.

"Quiet, remember," he demanded, and I collapsed against him, biting at his shoulder in my need not to scream.

Shuddering waves engulfed me, and I gave myself up to his controlling hands. One stayed, fingers kneading my ass, forcing me harder against his hard length, while the other caressed the back of my head, toying with my hair, brushing it away from my face.

The contrast, the hard and the soft, the caring and the commanding, captivated me until I shattered, thrashing against his chest.

Breath slowly returned as he stroked down the long lines of my back, heat following every movement of his fingers.

"Ready, love?"

Gently, as if I was made of glass, he rolled us until I lay beneath him, sprawled and dizzy.

And wanting.

I spread my legs wider, feet flat against the thin mattress, knees up, as the top of his broad cock inched its way into my slit.

"Iq'her," I gasped as tingles of pleasure shivered up my spine.

He froze.

"No, don't stop," I babbled, frantic.

Those amazing eyes crinkled at the corners as he panted. "That's good. I'm not sure if I could."

"Just don't let me…"

"How's this?" He shifted, one hand on my hip, the other arm resting on an elbow to the side of my head.

I turned my head slightly, into his broad palm.

Then licked it.

He drove into me, and I arched beneath him, pressing my mouth to his hand in earnest now as whatever control he'd maintained before broke.

Clamping me in place beneath him, he thrust harder, claiming me with every spark he sent through my body.

He leaned over me, breath hot in my ear, until there was nothing in the universe but him, my fingers clawing at his back, his cock pounding into my heat, his scent, his taste, his words in my ear, ringing through my mind.

My mate.

Mine.

There was no warning this time, no gradual build of the pleasure that crashed over me.

Just a shattering, a tearing apart of everything, until all I could do was cling to him, rocking with his pleasure and mine.

And yet, he still was not done. He kept pistoning in and out of me, taking me to another orgasm on the heels of the first one.

Delicious torment coursed through me as my fingers trembled and tears fell from my eyes. I lost the ability to breathe and think and just held on to Iq'her for safety as another orgasm ripped through me.

Then he stiffened, plunged into me even harder, and I felt his shuddering release deep within me.

Even when he was still, I lay trembling, body still wrapped in the aftershocks of what had passed between us.

As Iq'her collapsed next to me, we lay in silence for a while as I cuddled up next to him, then he carefully cleaned me, tucking me into the small bed that for just a short time had been our haven.

It was finally time for him to go.

Iq'her took a deep breath, dressed, and reactivated his holobelt. He was already by the door when he stopped in his tracks.

Looking back at me over his shoulder, he offered me a smile.

"One day we won't be hiding anything."

"That sounds wonderful."

A wicked grin lit his face.

"Stasia, *you'll* sound wonderful."

IQ'HER

I knew it was a nightmare, but I couldn't wake up from it.

I was picking my way over dead trees and plants everywhere; the entire planet was a wasteland. Animal bodies mixed with the vegetation. The sky was brown, the sun barely capable of sending its light through the miasma of smoke, dust, and death.

I was yelling out for anyone, anyone at all, to answer me. I saw no one. There was no one around me. I knew that couldn't have been right, there were people here, I just had to find them.

Then, out of the corner of my eye, I saw three people; Stasia, a smaller human, and Roddik.

Roddik was smiling from ear-to-ear. "I told you this

was all your fault. I told you that you were why we were dying."

Stasia was crying, and bleeding from a bad cut to her side. I yelled and ran to her, ripping my shirt off as I ran. I put the shirt against her to staunch the bleeding, but it didn't work. The harder I pressed, the more she bled.

"Why, Iq'her? Why? Why did you kill us?" she asked, her voice broken and hoarse.

"I didn't," I said back, except it wasn't my voice. My voice didn't sound like a power-mad maniac. My voice didn't sound like someone that had lost his mind.

"You did, Iq'her. You killed me. You killed our child." She looked down to the child whose hand she had been holding, and it was no longer a small human walking with her, but the body of a dead K'ver boy, his legs and feet dragging behind him.

"I'm sorry," I cried out. "I'm so sorry."

Their words kept repeating, over and over. "I told you this was your fault," and "Why did you kill us?" "You killed us." "Your fault." "Killed Us." "All your fault."

My dream-self screamed, a blood curdling scream that seemed to come more from a monster than it did from me.

There was an unusual crackling sound, and some broken words. They weren't part of my dream. I clung to those sounds, refusing to get sucked back into the whirlpool of nightmare.

I snapped awake, jumping out of the bed that I had been allowed to borrow by one of the villagers. I was breathing hard, my eyes wide and my mind racing. The dream had been so real.

There it was again, that crackling sound mixed with words.

Then, in sudden remembrance, I jumped back towards the bed and reached into my pack. The comm unit! The unit that I had stolen and set on *Vengeance's* frequency was going off.

I snatched it from my pack and fumbled with it, trying to get the volume. I found the volume controls and turned the radio down, afraid that it would be overheard by the humans in the room next door.

Forcing myself to calm down, I turned it up slightly and held it up to my ear.

"…essage." SHKRKK."ound…eam. Repe…is…ouhr and I…ved message fro…nd tea…ike t…s on way to l… ion…nowle…"

It was the general's voice. I listened carefully, but the words never came through correctly.

How was I going to…? I was interrupted mid-thought by shouts coming from outside. More shouts came, followed by some screams, and not just from outside. Someone, the lady of the house, shrieked an ear-splitting shriek that made me squint in pain.

I looked out my window to see the villagers and Roddik's crew racing around. It was chaotic outside. Then the house shook and something big and green blocked my window. Our old friend Puppet Master was back.

I grabbed my pack, my weapons were inside, and raced down the stairs. Halfway down, a vine crashed through the wall, catching me in the side and sending me careening into the far wall. I bounced off the wall with a huge thud, the air knocked from my lungs. Little stars and bursts of color erupted in front of my eyes, giving me the most amazing display of fireworks I could have ever hoped for.

Too bad the pain in my head and in my side ruined the whole moment. I grunted as I pushed myself to my knees. I could still hear shouting from upstairs, as well as from outside. The pain in my head would go away, but the pain in my side was constant, throbbing, a bit stabbing, actually.

I looked down to see a splinter the length and width of my thumb sticking out of my left side, a small circle of blood slowly growing in size around it.

I reached down and yanked it out, grunting loudly in pain as I did so. Not wanting to risk bleeding to death, I took out a small med kit I had hidden in the bottom of my bag. I wasn't supposed to bring my tech with me, but I had risked this. I took out a small spray can, opened up the straw at the end of it, stuck it into my wound with a hiss, and pressed down on the nozzle.

A gray foam came out of the canister and filled my wound, the tiny nano-mites inside the foam already starting on repairing any internal damage. This wasn't a fix-all that would repair me completely, but it was enough to prevent me from bleeding to death.

I put the canister back into my pack, retrieved the small handgun I had packed, and grabbed my knife. I ran outside to see vines sprouting out of the ground everywhere. I couldn't count how many vines there were, but there were only three of them that were large enough to take buildings down.

Everyone was outside, or almost everyone. I could still hear some shouts from behind me, back inside the house. Anyone with a weapon was attacking, trying to fight the vines, but whenever they attacked a vine, it turned its attention on them, swatting them away like tiny insects.

There were a few bodies on the ground, crumpled in unnatural positions. Even more were lying still on the ground or trying to slink away, moaning in pain. One of Roddik's main men was dragging himself away from an attacking vine, his right leg completely twisted backwards.

I rushed the vine, firing off a few shots before I stabbed down at it with my knife. My attack was about as successful as poking someone with a needle. I irritated the thing, possibly gave it a painful itch where my knife had stabbed it. My bullets had done more damage than my knife, they had given the thing something like an uncomfortable rash.

I was a warrior, damn it!

And I was in over my head. I dodged the vine as it swatted at me and cut at it again, this time using the cutting edge instead of the point. I cut into the vine.

By the stars, I finally cut into the vine! It—bled? secreted?—a pungent black liquid from the cut. It jerked back, then retreated back into the ground, only to be replaced by another vine. This one was smaller, but much faster.

By the time I managed to cut this one, I already had six welts and two cuts to my legs from it whipping me.

Then, there was a sudden rat-a-tat-tat of gunfire, much more gunfire than what this group had. Five transports landed in and around the village, all three strike teams, some human soldiers, and maybe a dozen members of various ground teams jumping out, weapons hot.

I was surprised to see General Rouhr leading the troops into battle. Vidia wouldn't be pleased.

However, I didn't have much time to celebrate their

arrival as my little whipping friend snapped across my back, the pain intense. I swiped at it, cutting off the top three feet of vine.

It retreated. I took a moment to breathe before jumping back into the fray.

STASIA

I was still asleep when the screaming started. Opening my eyes, I jumped out of bed fast. I rushed out of the bedroom, only to almost crash against Evna. The old woman was still bleary-eyed, but she didn't even pause as I stepped out of her way. She simply dashed toward the door and yanked it back.

"You've heard it, too, haven't ya?" she asked me, strain in her voice. The wrinkles in her face were now deeper with worry, and I could almost feel her frustration. Frail as she was, there was no way she'd be able to help if we were under attack.

"Yes, I've heard it," I replied, stepping outside and joining her by the garden. I had barely finished speaking when more screams echoed through the small town. "Go inside, Evna. And lock the doors. I'm going to see what's happening."

With a quiet nod, she did as I told her, but not before telling me to be careful. Even though she barely knew me, she seemed as if she was worried about me. As for me, I was worried about the whole town. Screams were never a good thing, no matter the situation, and with Roddik in town...who knew what could be happening?

The strike teams could be attacking, or Roddik could simply have gone ballistic and started shooting down civilians. Worse...the Xathi could be back.

Worst of all, Iq'her could be in trouble. Was he safe? He could take care of himself. I knew it, rationally.

"Keep it together, Stasia," I told myself as I ran down the street, hoping that I'd find the source of all the screaming. It was impossible—the moment I noticed panic on the other side of the street, more yells came from the other end of the settlement. In just a few seconds, it seemed as if everyone in town was screaming.

I froze in my tracks then, not knowing what to do, and that was when I felt the ground shift under my feet. There was a rumbling sound, one that made the hairs on the back of my neck stand up, and then a vine as thick as a tree trunk erupted from the earth. It reached higher and higher, and then it simply fell back down like a whip, cutting through the air as it went for one of the houses. It crashed against the roof with a loud noise, and only then did I realize who that house belonged to.

Alena and Uther.

"Crap," I muttered and, before I could even think twice about what I was about to do, I simply kicked the door open and rushed into the house. There was dust everywhere, and a lot of roof tiles had fallen on the kitchen counters and table. The beams that supported the roof were all starting to crack under the vine's weight, though, and it was only a matter of time before the whole house came crashing down.

"Stasia!" Alena cried out, coughing as she stumbled out of her bedroom. I went toward her right away and, grasping her waist with one hand, helped her get out of the house.

"Where's Uther?"

"He...he ran out the moment he heard the screams," she stammered, confusion stamped on her face. "He went to see what was going on, and that was when I heard a loud sound and then...the whole house shook... what is going on, Stasia?"

"It seems the vines are attacking us," I explained, even though I didn't know what any of it meant. "It happened before, in Nyheim." Still supporting her, I helped her walk down the street, guiding her toward

Evna's house. I wasn't sure if she would be safe there, but at least the two of them would be able to help each other if needed.

"Uther...I...I need to go see if he's fine," she tried to say, but I would have none of it.

"I'll go look for him," I promised her. "But right now, your baby is the priority, alright?"

She nodded at that, draping one protective arm over her large belly, and I breathed out with relief. It seemed like I wouldn't have to drag her toward Evna's, after all. Of course, getting her there wouldn't be easy.

Vines were sprouting from the ground every few feet or so, some of them moving as fast as whips and attacking everyone who dared stand in their way. Men were handled like ragdolls, thrown easily against the walls, and blades seemed to have little to no effect on the damn vines. That didn't surprise me—if the vines were strong enough to tear down walls, it was only obvious that they'd be hard to cut down. I just hoped these vines wouldn't be as hard as the ones that had entombed Nyheim...if that was the case, we'd be pretty screwed.

"We're almost there," I said, upping my pace as I saw Evna's house through the dust. Then, completely out of nowhere, the ground before us gave way and a vine jumped up in the air. It cracked like a whip before honing in on us, and I immediately pulled Alena back.

Gritting my teeth, I grabbed the hunting knife that hung from my belt and held my breath. No way in hell would I allow this stupid plant to hurt an innocent person. Only over my dead body would that happen.

Instead of striking right away, though, the vine simply hovered right in front of me. I was expecting it to attack me like a vicious predator, but its movements were elegant...almost as if there was some kind of intelligence at work. It was as if the vines were examining us, as crazy as that sounded.

I stood there completely still, not even daring to breathe, and then something crazy happened: just as quickly has it had sprouted, the vine slithered back to its hole in the ground. It reappeared behind us, but now much closer to the fight.

"Let's go!" I cried out, grabbing Alena's arm and dragging her after me. Neither of us said a word as we closed in on Evna's house, and I breathed out with relief as I saw that the vines had stayed clear of the old woman's place. Breathing hard, I hit the door with my fist repeatedly.

"Stasia?"

"Please, look after Alena," I said. Evna merely nodded, looking determined, and that was enough for me. I turned on my heels and returned to the center of the settlement, my fingers gripping the handle of my knife tightly.

It was chaos everywhere.

The vines were striking all men in a vicious manner, and there were a lot of unconscious bodies strewn across the small square. Iq'her was right in the thick of it, a gun in one hand and a knife in the other.

I called out his name, but the sound of my voice was drowned by the roar of loud engines. The wind whipped at my hair and, at the same time, large shadows covered the entirety of the square. I looked up to see five transport shuttles hovering over the settlement, their doors open as dozens of aliens clad in tactical gear rappelled down to the ground. They were frighteningly accurate, each shot they took hitting its target.

So, this was it.

Iq'her's endgame.

Not only had he managed to bring the strike teams, but there were also human soldiers in the fray. This time, Roddik wouldn't stand a chance. Of course, none of the newcomers seemed concerned with Roddik and his goons...their only concerns were the vines.

But then, when all the troops had reached the ground, the impossible happened.

Of their own accord, the vines simply started retreating, slithering back to the holes they had opened when they broke onto the surface. Everyone—friends and foes alike—simply watched it happen, surprise the one emotion on people's faces.

"Men!" A tall green Valorni bellowed, pointing straight at Roddik. "Remember why we're here. The criminal, Roddik!"

Roddik's face turned pale the moment he heard his name, and his eyes grew wide with panic. He dropped his gun to the ground and tried to make a run for it, but he didn't get far — one of the Valorni tackled him and subdued him, producing a pair of handcuffs from his belt and using them on Roddik's wrists.

"No! No! No!" Roddik cried out as he saw his group surrendering. Moving like a well-oiled machine, the aliens had every member of Roddik's original group in handcuffs in less than a minute. "You fucking beasts! I'll kill you all!"

"No, you won't," Iq'her said, standing right in front of Roddik. Looking straight into my brother's eyes, he turned off his holobelt, revealing his true appearance. "Not on my watch."

"Ilkay…?"

"The name's Iq'her."

"You fucking alien scum," my brother continued to scream, even when one of the Valorni dragged him toward the shuttle. It pained me to see him like that, but I knew it needed to happen.

My brother was dangerous, and he needed to be

stopped. I realized with how strongly I felt for Iq'her --
safe and happy -- that my brother was the toxic, lethal
opposite.

"Stasia, you alright?" Iq'her asked me, reaching for
me and laying one hand on my face. "I was so worried
about you."

"I'm fine," I smiled, resting my hand on top of his.
"It's over, isn't it?"

"It is," he said. "We can go home now."

IQ'HER

It wasn't the most cheerful flight back to Nyheim. In order to ensure that the prisoners didn't attempt to take over any particular transport, they were spread out amongst them all, which meant that there were about eight humans—not counting Stasia—on the transport that I was on with my team and Rouhr.

I looked at the people, only two of them were from Roddik's original group. The other six were villagers that had taken arms up against us. *There's just too many of them, even without the villagers,* I thought. We weren't going to have enough room to house them all.

Our transports were not the best vehicles possible for quiet conversation. The air that whooshed through it meant that we would have to speak up in order to be heard, even with comms. I tried to speak where only the general would hear me. "We don't have enough room for all of the prisoners, if they remain prisoners, sir."

He nodded and turned to me, his voice just as loud as mine. "I know. What do you suggest?"

I hadn't thought that far ahead. There were a few buildings in the city proper that were large enough, but they weren't properly outfitted. And, to be honest, the prospect of having a large group of prisoners within city limits was never a good idea. If they ever escaped, there was an entire city full of potential hostages, and this group had already shown me that taking hostages wasn't far from their level of thinking.

So that meant we would have to imprison them outside the city. The only places I could think of were the old quake stations. Some of them were massive and had lots of rooms. They wouldn't take long to refit. Of course, they would have to be fenced or walled off eventually and have a housing area created for the prison guards, as well as other logistical issues. But it was the best idea I could come up with.

"What about the quake stations, sir?" I suggested. "There's a lot of logistical items that would need to be handled, but they would be far away from civilization and wouldn't be a danger." Of course, by placing them that far away, they could be seen as martyrs that were sent away just because we disagreed with their mentality.

To solidify that thought, one of the humans from the original group spoke up. "That's right, send us away. It proves you're scared of us and what we stand for." I looked at the one that spoke. He was one of the bigger men, with a terrible four-day stubble that he was trying to grow into a beard. A scar ran down his right arm from his shoulder to his elbow. He was also missing a few teeth, so it was hard for me to consider him as terribly intelligent.

I'm automatically judging someone based on their looks, just like those foolish humans are.

"We're not scared of what you represent. I actually empathize with you a bit. There's a couple of races out in the universe that I don't like, either, because of how they are," I explained. "So, I can understand a little bit of what you're feeling. But you need to understand that we're trying to make amends for the damage that was caused by our arrival with the Xathi."

"And I would be grateful for the help, *if* you bothered to do it our way instead of yours," he spat back. "But you don't want to. You think you know better, and you leave us out. You take our food, you take our women, you take our homes and think that you're better than us."

"That's not true," Rouhr said. "I have been getting

the advice of humans during this entire process. We all have to live together."

Before Bad-Beard could talk again, one of the villagers spoke. "What's happening, then? Why don't you tell us that?"

"Well," I said, taking the conversation over. "After we crash landed here, fought the Xathi, and eventually defeated them, something odd started happening with some of the more sentient plant creatures." I went on to explain what happened that led to Tella eventually becoming part of the team, as well as the massive vines that completely enclosed the city.

"Eventually, one of my team members, partnering with a human woman, found something that was able to eliminate the vines that were imprisoning the city," I continued explaining. "However, soon after the vines fell, reports began to come in that the plants we *all* use were dying. That's the reasoning behind the food rationing mandate."

The villagers seemed to take our answer, but Bad-Beard wasn't buying it. "Lies!" he yelled out. "How do we know that what you're telling us is the truth? How do we know that all of this information is real? What if you're making it up to cover up what you're really doing?"

I took the bait, "What are we doing that we have to cover up?"

"You're killing off our food so we'll be too weak to fight back," he started. "Then you'll take over and take those of us that don't immediately follow you blindly and throw us away, or kill us. Hell, you're already taking us to jail and talking about doing it someplace really far away."

His friend from the group had looked on the fence about everything, now he was back on Bad-Beard's side. The part that scared me was that two of the villagers were talking to one another and were nodding along with Bad-Beard's accusations.

I opened my mouth to respond, but Rouhr grabbed my shoulder. A shake of his head told me not to respond anymore, so I clamped my mouth shut.

"I was right, wasn't I? That's why you won't let him talk, huh? I fucking knew it!" For the rest of the trip back to Nyheim, Bad-Beard continued with his diatribe, throwing accusations, stories, and lies at us.

When we landed, General Rouhr directed Teams One and Three and the ground teams to escort the humans to our small detention center where they would be held until we could figure out where to put them.

"Keep the villagers apart from the others," I suggested. "They weren't part of the attack."

Rouhr nodded at me. "Good point. Do it," he said to the others, then turned back to me. "Let's talk."

"Hey, hey!" I heard Stasia shouting.

I looked back to see Axtin grabbing her, gently for how big he was.

"No, not her. She wasn't part of the attack, either," I said.

"She was on the video," Axtin countered.

I glared at him. "She. Wasn't. Part. Of. The. Attack." I repeated slowly. "She was dragged along by her brother. She wasn't a willing participant."

Axtin looked past me to Rouhr and Karzin. I assumed they both nodded or some other signal that told him to let her go.

He released her and I held my hand out to her.

She came over and took my hand, holding on so tight it almost hurt.

We followed Rouhr back to his office. He asked for my report, so I explained to him what had happened; how I had tracked them down, how the plants and vegetation were present when we first made camp, then were dying or dead the next day, how there were no animals to be found, and how Roddik and his inside people had come up with the idea of taking over the settlement instead of simply joining it.

Stasia confirmed my report and made her own report as well, albeit a bit hesitantly.

"Understood," Rouhr said. "As to your idea for using one of the quake stations, it's not a bad idea. My only concern is how long it would take to refit the place and construct some sort of barrier around it so no one would be able to escape."

"We could always make the prisoners build the wall," Karzin said.

"Oh, that'll go over well with the humans that hold sympathy towards them," I snapped, instantly regretting it. "My apologies for my tone, Commander."

"Forgiven," Karzin said. "Then what do you suggest? Even if we commission the work and have the work paid for, any humans associated with the project will know that it's a prison for humans."

"Why does it have to be just for humans?" Stasia asked.

I laid my hand on hers. "Think about it. The first people that will be imprisoned there hate us," I moved my hand to indicate the non-humans in the office. "If we were to throw a non-human in there with them, we're basically assigning them to death."

"Then what do we do?" she asked me. I didn't have an answer.

"Do you want to administer it?" Rouhr asked me.

"Me? Run the prison?" Surprisingly, it held a bit of appeal to me. I could institute programs and work-orders that would be used to help change the prisoners, get them to see that we weren't bad people. Maybe even get them to learn some skills, or augment the ones they already had, and help them become more productive to society as a whole.

"No, thank you, sir. I'd rather stay here."

"Why?"

I looked at Stasia. "I want to help prove that she wasn't a willing part of this, that she only went along because she was trying to keep a promise to her parents. And I want to work with her on trying to improve relations between all of us."

Stasia smiled a thank you at me.

There was no way I could leave that smile.

"Are you sure this is fine?" I asked, hesitantly stepping inside.

The large family next door to my old apartment was spilling over, far too many people crammed into a small space.

With memories of Roddik haunting me at every turn, it had been a relief when Iq'her suggested I stay at his place for a while, let them have the extra space. When I wanted to move on, I could. Someplace better for one person. Someplace with fewer memories.

I thought it was a good idea when he had said it, but now, standing in the middle of his living room, I wasn't so sure anymore.

I didn't want to be a nuisance, especially since I knew Iq'her was awfully busy.

"Of course it is fine." He closed the door behind him and offering me a wide smile. "In fact, it's more than just fine. I'm happy you've decided to stay here with me. Being by myself all the time… it gets lonely."

"I know that feeling," I whispered, sinking onto his couch.

Even though I had been living with Roddik before everything went to hell, I still felt completely alone. In fact, whenever Roddik used to be in the apartment, I felt even lonelier. His presence had been disquieting, a reminder of my failure as his sister.

"I've let everybody down," I continued, biting down on my bottom lip. I had been running on pure adrenaline the past few days, but now reality was slowly starting to sink in. "My brother, my parents… I've failed everyone. "

"Stasia—"

"Maybe I deserve to be arrested. Roddik got so lost in his ways because of me… had I been stronger, maybe he wouldn't have turned out the way he did." I looked down at my feet, feeling that hollowness in my heart growing with each word I said. "This is all my fault, Iq'her."

"None of this is your fault," he tried to calm me, sitting next to me. He turned around on the couch so that he was facing me, and then placed two fingers under my chin. Forcing me to look into his eyes, he continued, "You did the best you could, Stasia. In fact, you did so much more than what Roddik deserved… he didn't care for you, and that's the truth. He never deserved a great sister like you are."

"Will he be okay?" I couldn't stop myself from asking. "In prison, I mean."

"Yes, he will," he replied in a heartbeat. "I'm going to make sure our prison system works. I don't want it to be punishment. Whoever we send to prison, I want to make sure they have a chance at redemption."

"You're a good man, Iq'her."

Breathing out softly, I laid my head on his shoulder. His presence was soothing in an inexplicable way… but I didn't care for an explanation, anyway. All I knew was that I needed to have him around me. Inside me. I wanted to be consumed by him.

In a way, Iq'her was now the only family I had left.

"I try to be." He drew me into a tight but gentle embrace. I fell into his arms willingly, relishing the warmth of his body. "And whenever I'm with you… it makes me want to be even better."

"I like that." I nodded, pushing myself off him just so I could look into his eyes. "I feel exactly the same."

He smiled at that, and I just appreciated the way he did it.

He was so much more handsome without the holobelt, his alien features exotic and alluring. He wasn't as tall as some of his race, but, on the other hand, his body seemed more balanced than bulky. His athletic features gave him an air of agility despite his size, and I had seen up close just how strong he was.

"It's time we have a chance to make noises we couldn't before," I found myself saying, my heart beating faster. Standing up, I pulled my blouse over my head and unclasped my bra. Iq'her's eyes went wide as his gaze took in the shape of my round breasts, and I couldn't help but notice the hard shape that immediately tented his pants.

"Sounds like a good idea," he grinned, slowly getting to his feet.

I closed in on him, pressing my naked breasts against his chest, and helped him remove his shirt. I took a moment to run my fingers over the contours of his muscles, but then allowed desire to guide my movements — I went down on my knees in front of him and, hooking my fingers in the waistband of his pants, I tugged them down to his ankles.

"I want to see all of you," I whispered as he kicked off his boots and pants. Holding my breath, I pulled his underwear down, freeing his erection, his hard cock springing free immediately. It was bigger than I had imagined it to be, and I couldn't resist but lean into it right away, my tongue going from its tip to the base. "I want to taste all of you."

I took my time as I savored him, and only changed gears when he laid both hands on my head. The moment I felt the touch of his fingers, I opened my mouth wide and rolled my lips down his whole length, only stopping when I could feel him against the back of my throat.

"Stasia…" he groaned, his voice brimming with pleasure.

To know that I was the reason behind his pleasure was more than I could've wished for, and it just made me go harder. I bobbed my head up and down as fast as I could, pleasuring him with my mouth, savoring the scale and shape of his cock, and I only stopped when he took a step back. "I want more of you," he growled, reaching down to hold my hand.

Pulling me up to my feet, he pushed me back until I was pinned between his body and the wall. "I want *all* of you."

"Then what are you waiting for? I'm right here for the taking."

He didn't reply to that.

He paused for a moment, looking straight at me, and I saw hunger burning bright in his eyes. Before I even knew what was happening, he had already stripped the pants off my body. My heart pounded fiercely against my chest as he removed the final obstacle between both our bodies, my underwear, and I let out a quivering moan as the cool air of the room caressed my wetness.

"You're perfect, Stasia." Leaning in, he brushed his lips against mine, teasing me. "I want to make you mine."

"And I want to be yours," I whispered against his lips, reaching down to grab his hardness. I curled my fingers tightly around his cock, and he reacted fast: grabbing me by the waist, he pulled me up and into him. I laced my legs around his waist and, letting go of his hard, ribbed cock, threw both arms over his shoulders.

I held my breath as I felt the enormous tip of his cock pressed against my entrance, and then rested my forehead on his chest as I readied myself for what was about to happen.

One thrust and he was in.

His cock was so large that I still couldn't imagine how he had fit, even after taking him before, but I was so eager to have him that he easily slid deep inside me. I felt my inner walls struggle to accommodate him, but that just amplified the pleasure I was feeling, every ridge bringing me closer to ecstasy.

"Harder," I begged him, and he gave me exactly what I needed. He started pistoning into me at a frantic pace, his tongue now dancing in a frenzy around one of my nipples, and I felt as if my body was burning from the inside out.

I had never experienced anything so amazing before and, now that I had had a taste, I was pretty sure I was going to become an addict.

"So fucking good," he growled, driving his cock deeper inside me with each of his thrusts. It didn't take long for my whole body to start tensing up, my inner walls gripping his cock as tightly as a vise. My eyes rolled back as my mind stuttered, unable to keep up with processing each sensation that flared through me.

"Iq'her!" I screamed at the top of my lungs, the bliss I was feeling turning into sound.

He simply kept on thrusting as I came, the fury of his movements making me moan even louder, but it didn't take long before he was breathing as hard as I was, his burning gaze letting me know he was about to explode.

"Stasia…" He groaned, thrusting one final time before he finally surrendered. He held still for a moment, his body pressed against mine, and I felt his hardness throb violently inside me, his warm seed filling me up.

Neither of us moved or said a thing.

We just remained perfectly still, Iq'her holding me up against the wall as I held tight to his body. We were reeling from something we had never experienced before, a kind of connection that revealed what I had known all along: I would never let go of Iq'her.

No matter what happened, we had to stay together.

"Stay with me..." I whispered, voicing my thoughts.

Pushing a lock of hair away from my face, Iq'her smiled.

"Always, Stasia...always."

IQ'HER

There was a palpable change in the city since our return. There were dozens of people around when we landed, and they had seen us take Roddik and his people out of the transports.

Not to mention that many of the villagers had been released. While we had helped get them back home and sent crews out to help them rebuild and repair, they had insisted on human crews.

We were losing ground in our relations with the humans.

Sylor was still friends with the restaurant owners where he ate, but some of the wait-staff refused to serve him, even though they knew him.

They had never minded before.

I used to frequent a small store filled with various

parts and pieces of technology, often times helping the staff inside fix, repair, or build something new. Now, I was told to only be there in the evenings, and only a few nights a week.

While there had always been several humans that seemed wary to be around us, now they were open in their dislike of us.

Too much was happening far too fast.

One of the crews that we had commissioned to begin construction of the wall around the quake station we had chosen to be the prison had quit and each member, along with their families, moved to the coastal city of Kaster.

If they spread their story there, Kaster would soon start to turn against us. It was the only city untouched by our battle with the Xathi, but they knew about it. Many refugees had moved there.

I tried to go out of my way to be nice to the humans, all of us did. Well, almost all of us. Karzin was still his surly self, but the surly self that he was since Annie's arrival. Even our human friends spoke up on our behalf.

But the feelings of Roddik and his people spread, like a wildfire during a drought.

Early this morning, there had been a fight between nearly a dozen people, separated by their opinions of us.

The humans that were supportive of us were attacked, several of them injured. When one of the ground crews working the overnight patrol broke it up, they were forced to used violence and three of the antagonists were injured and ended up at the hospital.

A report came in an hour ago that those three had to be moved to an empty section of the hospital to stop them from yelling at everyone they saw and heard.

I sat in my office, my head in my hands as I tried to figure out what was happening. I knew that we would never get all of the humans to like us, but we had gone months without open hatred directed at us. It had given me hope that things were going to be at least civil.

Who could have predicted that a person such as Roddik would the catalyst for a human revolt against their own people and us? Yes, we were doing many things across the continent, but we were doing it with the permission of humans in an attempt to make their lives better.

We were trying to help, trying to fix what had been damaged and, in many cases, upgrade or improve on those things. It wasn't our fault that we had better technology and a better understanding of how many things worked.

So what if we were taking command of many of the recovery efforts? We knew how the damage was done and knew how to undo that damage. Why shouldn't we have been in charge, at least of those efforts?

We weren't trying to control the cities. Rouhr wasn't in control of Nyheim, he was an advisor. Of course, he was an advisor with the capabilities and permission to order people around, so I guess I could see how people would misconstrue that into thinking he was in charge.

As Leena and Tella would say... God fucking dammit! We had to find other ways of figuring this out and making it work.

"Iq'her?"

I picked my head up to see Tobias standing in the doorway.

"I'm sorry to bother you, but another runner came in with a report," he said meekly and placed the report on my desk.

As he turned to leave, I asked "Do you think we're trying to take things over, Tobias?"

He stopped in the doorway. I could see his shoulders drop a bit. "I know why you're asking." He turned to me, a sad look on his face. "I don't believe you're trying to take over or control us, but I'm only one person. There's a lot of people that do feel that way."

I nodded. "I know. How do we fix that?"

"I don't know." He stepped back into my office. "I've been kicked out of my apartment because of my affiliation with all of you. My landlord doesn't feel that it's good for him and the rest of his tenants to have such a 'blatant alien lover' living in his building."

That hurt me, right in my heart. "I'm sorry, Tobias. You don't deserve that kind of treatment."

"Thank you for thinking so, sir," he said, a weak smile on his face. "It's okay, though. I've always wanted to move over by the park and the pond anyway. Much more tranquil view, if you ask me."

I nodded. "I agree. If you come up with any ideas on how we can improve relationships between all of us, please don't keep it to yourself."

"I won't. I firmly believe that all of you are only trying to help, and I appreciate that." He stepped out of my office, closing the door behind him.

I picked up the report and read through it. It was about the attack this morning. The three sent to the hospital had four more with them, two of which escaped. The night patrol that had dealt with them had gone back to their bunkhouse.

While there, the bunkhouse was attacked by people throwing rocks, pipes, anything heavy.

Three of our own injured, one badly thanks to a rock to the eye, and significant property damage.

What the skrell were we to do?

"How do I look?"

"Perfect," Iq'her smiled. Grabbing my hand, he forced me to do a quick twirl and then leaned down to kiss my forehead. "Don't worry. You're going to do great."

"If you say so," I whispered, not knowing what to think. I wasn't feeling as confident as he was, that was for sure.

A few days ago, I was nothing but a waiter, and now here I was... ready to meet the Nyheim mayor and General Rouhr. Of course, I requested for Iq'her to accompany me, since I would feel more comfortable with him around.

All my life I had been adrift, but with him by my side... everything felt just right.

I could be strong, knowing that he'd always have my back. And now, I needed to go tell some very scary people, some very scary things.

"The general and the mayor are ready to see you now," a young secretary announced, gesturing toward the large double doors in front of us.

She pushed them open and then stepped out of the way to allow us in. I did my best to keep a straight posture as I marched inside the office, holding Iq'her's hand so tightly I was surprised he wasn't complaining.

"Miss Stasia Cole, I presume," the general greeted me. He was sitting behind a large desk in the center of the office, but he stood up the moment I stepped inside the room. He offered me his hand and I took it, barely believing that I was shaking hands with the alien responsible for the city. "I'm the general, but I believe you already know that."

"And I'm Vidia Birch," the woman standing next to the general said, a kind smile on her lips. "But I believe you know that, as well. Thank you so much for taking the time, Miss Cole."

"Please… it's Stasia."

"Stasia," the general smiled. He gestured toward the empty chair in front of his desk and I sat down on it, already trying to think of everything I needed to say.

After the chaos that my brother had unleashed, both the general and the mayor had decided they couldn't remain idle while the city population split itself down the middle.

They wanted to bridge the gap between the different races and, for that to happen, they needed to hear from me.

"Are you nervous, Stasia?" Vidia asked me, and I found myself nodding.

"Don't be," she smiled, laying a hand on my shoulder. "We're among friends here. We wanted to meet with you because of everything you went through… your experience is invaluable. I know that the people have been complaining about the way we've handled things so far, and we want to hear what those complaints are. We want to do better, and that's how we'll start."

"I want to help, too," I told her, and then took a deep breath before continuing.

I started out slowly, going through whatever it was I remembered people in the street constantly complained about, but my arguments started becoming clearer and clearer with each word that left my mouth.

The government needed to be more transparent about its dealings, and it was important for the population to know the aliens were only acting in an advisory capacity. If people stopped seeing the aliens as usurpers, that would be a start.

It wouldn't be easy, but I trusted that people would

come to their senses sooner or later. Hope needed to triumph over despair, and I would do my best to keep on believing.

"Those are some great insights," the general mused when I was finally done. I only realized I had been speaking nonstop for almost twenty minutes when I felt the need to reach for some water, my mouth completely dry. "You have your finger on this city's pulse, Stasia."

"I wouldn't go that far, sir. I'm just an ordinary person."

"Don't sell yourself short," he said kindly. "More often than not, the common people are the ones that change the course of history. Tell me, Stasia, how would you like to serve as a special liaison between the government and the people?"

"I... what?"

"It'd only be a temporary position," Vidia smiled. "At least at first. But the people need to see they have someone on their side. Someone who they can trust to voice their concerns, and someone that'll keep them in the loop. After everything you've gone through, I believe you're the right person for the job."

"I will do my best." I straightened my back. It was a big responsibility, one that I was almost afraid to accept, but if I could help Nyheim be a better place...then it was my duty to do so. "Thank you for believing in me."

"Well, you came extremely well recommended." General Rouhr laughed, and I couldn't help but notice that he exchanged a quick glance with Iq'her.

"Thank you." Getting up from my seat, I looked from Rouhr to Vidia. "Not only for trusting me... but for being so open about everything. I wasn't sure before, but now I know that the right people are in charge."

"We're glad to hear it, Stasia."

Feeling more optimistic about the future than I had felt in weeks, I started walking toward the door, Iq'her by my side. I already had one foot outside the office when I suddenly remembered something.

"There's something else," I started, turning on my heels to face both the general and the mayor. "It's about the vines... they behaved strangely during the fight in the settlement."

"Strangely? How?"

"One of the vines seemed as if it was about to attack me, but then... it stopped. I don't know what happened, or why it was acting like that, but I can't help but think it was watching me. *Examining* me. Somehow, I don't think that the vines are just plants."

"No, they're more than just plants," Rouhr agreed.

"But what you're describing is new. What happened after?"

"Instead of attacking me and the woman I was with, the vine... it simply retreated. I have no idea why, but it was almost as if it didn't want to attack me. It *thought* about it, and then *decided* against it. At least that's what I believe, General."

"Thank you for sharing that with us," he said solemnly, his smile from before replaced by a serious expression. "We'll pass that information along immediately."

With one final nod, I turned around and left.

"I knew you were going to do great." Iq'her laughed as we made our way out of the building. "I just had no idea that you'd dazzle them like you did."

"I didn't dazzle anyone," I protested.

"Trust me, I've known the general for years now... and he definitely looked impressed. He nominated you as a special liaison, Stasia. That's irrefutable proof that you impressed the man."

"There's only one man I want to impress," I laughed, stopping right before we left the building. Turning to Iq'her, I went up on tiptoes and kissed him. "And that man is you."

EPILOGUE: STASIA

That night, Iq'her and I went up to the rooftop. His apartment building was one of the tallest in Nyheim, and the view from the rooftop was incredible. The sky above us was littered with thousands of tiny burning stars, and the city itself seemed to reflect the vaulted night sky, the dim lights of the streets illuminating the city arteries.

Nyheim was one of the largest cities on the planet, and even at night it seemed to bustle with life. Even despite all the hardships, the city's spirit had remained strong and unbowed.

Unbroken.

"It's funny, but I never really took the time to appreciate Nyheim," I said as I leaned against the railing, my elbows resting on the cold steel. "I had always taken it for granted, I guess."

"It's a beautiful city, yes," Iq'her whispered, almost as if he was afraid to disturb the night's quietness. Closing the distance between us, he laid one hand on my waist. "But, more important than that, this our home."

"Home."

The word was as simple as it was beautiful but, at the same time, it sounded almost foreign. Exotic, even. After my parents' deaths, I never really thought I'd feel at home again, no matter the place I ended up. Then Iq'her stepped into my life, and he showed me just how wrong I was.

"Yes, home," he repeated. "It has its problems, but we'll help turn it into a better place. In time, Nyheim will flourish."

"I believe you."

It was the truth. I had always been a pessimist, but that had already started to change. There was hope in my heart, not to mention that I also felt responsible for the city's future. A public liaison role wasn't much, but it was a start. I now had a purpose, and I would do my best to ensure I would make a difference, no matter how little it'd be.

"Stasia," Iq'her spoke up after a short moment. "There's something I've been thinking about these past few days."

"Something good, I hope," I said as I turned to face him, an amused smile spreading across my lips. He seemed nervous, and that was an emotion I wasn't used to seeing on his face.

"I hope so," he nodded. "I hope this isn't too sudden, but… will you move in with me? Stay here, forever?"

For a moment, I said nothing. I just stared into his big eyes, my heart happily beating inside my chest, then I threw myself at him. "YES!" I cried out. Smiling, he picked me up easily with both hands on my hips, and spun me around.

By the time my feet touched the floor, I was elated.

My body felt frail and delicate against his, and right then and there I realized just how much I really *needed* him.

Without him, I would never be whole again.

"Come here," I whispered.

My eyelids slid half closed as my lips parted for him, and he tasted me as if this was our first kiss all over again. Our lips didn't linger on each other for long, but when he pulled back there was a fire in his eyes.

He let his fingers go from my cheek to the nape of my neck, and softly tangled them in my hair. "I love you, Stasia." His words hit me with the force of a thousand burning suns and, for a moment, I was speechless.

Then I realized I wanted to say the same.

In fact, I desperately needed to hear me say it out loud. Only then would I know that what we had was real, that it wasn't a dream I would wake up from.

"And I love you, Iq'her."

He smiled then, and pulled me close. "Come," he said, holding my hand. "Like you humans say... this deserves a celebration."

"It does," I laughed, my heart tightening as I anticipated what he had in mind. It wasn't hard to predict, since I had the same exact thing on my mind. Iq'her and I... we were completely in sync.

We had barely made it through the door of his apartment when our lips met, the magnetic pull between the two of us too strong to resist. Kissing in a frenzy, we stumbled our way through the apartment, discarding our clothes as we went. By the time we collapsed on top of his bed, our naked bodies were already burning from the inside out, desperate for each other.

"Take me," I begged him, wrapping my legs around his waist as he loomed above me. Laying his body on top of mine, he pressed the tip of his cock against my entrance and teased me. His eyes remained on mine and the smile on his face was a defiant one. "I said, take me... *now*."

With that, I tightened my legs around his waist and pulled him into me as hard as I could. Unable to resist, he sheathed the whole length of his erection deep inside me, and I arched my back as pleasure shot up my spine. I didn't even know if I was moaning or screaming… all I knew was that my throat was growing raw, and that every single nerve ending on my body had suddenly come alive.

We tumbled into an abyss of pleasure together, our hands exploring each other's bodies as we surrendered to the passion. In those minutes, we were in a place that was outside of time, somewhere only we knew. The real word had remained shut outside, and even all the memories that still haunted me faded away temporarily.

For those moments, only Iq'her and I existed.

"I love you… so much," I repeated, enjoying the way these words rolled off my tongue so damn easily. "And as long as you love me, I'll never let go."

"Then you'll never let go," he whispered between thrusts, "because I'll never stop loving you."

I wasn't sure if the cause was his movements or his words, but something inside me flared up all of a sudden. Electricity shot up my spine, my eyes rolled back in their orbits, and I grabbed the sheets underneath me so hard that I almost ripped the fabric apart. Iq'her groaned at the same time, his hardness throbbing furiously inside me, and then…

"Iq'her!"

"STASIA!"

We exploded at the same time, our voices blending into a symphony of pure ecstasy. My blood felt as if it was boiling inside my veins, and even my thoughts seemed to have turned into liquid.

Right then, I was nothing but a vessel to pleasure.

"That was incredible," I breathed out a few minutes later when Iq'her rolled to the side. We remained sprawled on the mattress for a long time, simply staring at the ceiling while we both tried to catch our breaths.

I couldn't tell if it happened by chance or on purpose, but my hand brushed against his and, without even thinking about it, we intertwined our fingers. Just like our lives were now intertwined.

"It was more than incredible, Stasia. It was… perfect."

"Thanks to you," I chuckled softly, and then propped myself up on one elbow. "What happens now, Iq'her? We're together, but Nyheim still needs us."

"And we'll do what we can," he said. "Meanwhile…we'll just have to follow the plan."

"And what's the plan?"

"To be happy," he smiled.

That's easy, I thought to myself. *As long as I have you, happiness is a given.*

I THINK *it probably says a lot that one of my biggest childhood crushes was on Spock. Because my K'ver warriors, always so logical, seem to fall the hardest :)*

Next up, we're back to the threat that lies under the earth...

NOSY, undisciplined humans aren't high on his list. Not until a brilliant, beautiful doctor sets all his senses on fire.

LIVING with his brother Rokul and his human mate Tella was quite enough for Takar.

A life in the military taught him to be controlled. Restrained.

Rules were there for a reason, even if the humans never seemed to understand.

But when a curious human woman bursts into his duty station, he can't get escape his thoughts of her.

And when she plunges into danger, he'll ignore his own rules to keep his mate safe.

SCIENTIST DAPHNE IS terrible with mysteries. She wants to know everything about, well, everything.

The world is filled with questions, and she wants the answers.

When Takar is sent to retrieve her from a slightly unauthorized research trip, she's beyond annoyed.

But when they're trapped in the tunnels, she realizes she has just as many questions about the gruff Skotan warrior.

Who is he, really? How does his touch send heat through her belly? And why does she want to run her hands across his broad chest...and more?

KEEP READING FOR A SNEAK PEEK, or get it on Amazon now!

XOXO,

Elin

D aphne

"YOU LOOK LIKE A HUNGRY VALORNI," Annie laughed, watching as I went through my serving of noodles and thinly-sliced cuts of Luurizi meat.

"No," I protested with a mouthful, frowning as I eyed the tiny portion on her plate. "You're the one who's barely eating. Are you on a diet or something?"

"No, I just eat like a regular human being."

"It's not my fault the food is so damn good in here," I continued, barely stopping to breath as I devoured whatever was left on my plate. I exhaled deeply then, leaning back against my seat and feeling completely satisfied.

Biher's was a small restaurant located right between the main government building and Nyhiem's hospital, where I had met Annie.

The restaurant was conveniently located between our two places of work, and we were both fans of the food in there. Sure, food shortages sometimes wreaked havoc on the menu, but the place's atmosphere made up for that. Both aliens and humans ate here, no animosity between the two groups, and it felt like the perfect hiding spot from the growing tensions in the city.

"So, what's new?" I asked Annie, checking the holoscreen on the wall. I still had time before I had to be back at work, which meant I could pepper her with questions. There weren't any major surgeries planned for the afternoon, so I wouldn't be needed in the operating theatres.

"Same old," she smiled, fending off my question for the hundredth time. Luckily for me, she never grew tired of my non-stop questions. Curiosity was part of my DNA, after all, and Annie accepted that quirk of mine easily.

Of course, that just made me even more relentless in my pursuit of answers.

"Rocks, rocks, and then some more rocks. A thrilling day in a geologist's life."

"Oh, come on, Annie," I protested. "You gotta give me more than that. You're working under the Mayor and General Rouhr. You must be working on something more interesting than just rocks. You could be analyzing the materials from the Xathi site, or you could be working on some geological samples that came on the *Vengeance*."

"It's nothing like that," she laughed, but I just kept pestering her with even more questions. That was my defining trait: whenever I started with the questions, I would never stop.

While it annoyed my parents to no end when I was growing up, it also ensured I had been curious enough to pursue a career in the neurosciences. Still, while work at the hospital was interesting—I helped out on surgeries while still conducting my research on the side —it wasn't enough for me. I always needed to know more about the world around me...and, after the aliens' arrival on the planet, that hunger for more had only grown exponentially.

"Alright, alright," she surrendered, holding both hands up. "I'm working on something you'd love, but I really can't say much."

"Is it a confidential project?"

"You know it."

"Crap. No clues?"

"Nope," she smiled. "The only thing I can say is that it's something so weird I'm pretty sure you'd love it."

I paused at that, going through all the possible

scenarios in my mind. There were a lot of areas where Annie's work could make a difference but, since she was working under the General, it had to be something of relevance to the government.

And it if wasn't connected to the Xathi or to something that had come from outside the planet...then it could only mean Annie was working on something that was happening right now, on this planet.

"You're working on the vines, aren't you?" I exclaimed, a wave of excitement running through me. The vines were probably one of the most interesting subjects a scientist could be studying right now, no doubt about that.

Too bad I was sitting on the sidelines, completely clueless to what was going on.

"How did you know?" She started, frowning as she realized I had seen through her. "I'm not supposed to talk about this without anyone, you know?"

"My lips are sealed," I said, pretending I was locking them up with an imaginary key I immediately flung off. "Just tell me what's the angle on this. Are you testing it for measurable signs of intelligence? Or even sentience? What kind of biometric readings are you using?"

"Look, I don't know much," she finally relented, a more serious expression on her face. "And even if I did, it's not like I'd be able to tell you. The only thing I might say is that the higher-ups call this...*thing*...the Puppet Master."

"The Puppet Master?"

"Lower your voice," she hissed, leaning forward and scanning the room with her eyes. No one seemed particularly concerned with our conversation, but I still mouthed an apology. "I don't wanna get in trouble. Everyone's already freaking out with how little they know, and the last thing they want is everyone in the city freaking out too."

"Is there any reason for people to freak out?"

"Hello? Remember the way the vines tore the city apart? Or how we were trapped inside that dome? If that isn't enough for people to freak out about this Puppet Master, then I don't know what to tell you."

"Point taken," I nodded, a thousand thoughts already taking over my mind. Annie wasn't giving me much, but it was all so fascinating. "It's just that...well, there weren't that many casualties, were there? And the buildings that got destroyed, I somehow doubt they were targeted at random."

"What's that supposed to mean?" she asked, forehead creased.

"Well, the industrial precinct was the place with most destroyed buildings. Do you think that's a coincidence? Because to me it looks like it happened deliberately. This thing, whatever it is, isn't just some dumb plant. There's real intelligence behind it."

Of course, I didn't have any proof to back what I was saying, but my gut was telling me that I was right. And, more often than not, my instincts had a tendency to be correct.

"That's...interesting," she hesitated over her words. "I hadn't considered that there could be a real pattern, although I agree with you that this thing has some kind of intelligence. Not that it matters much...there's little to no funding to conduct an investigation. And, to make matters worse, we're short-staffed. Everyone's just so damn busy trying to prevent more incidents, or at least ensuring we're ready for them."

"That's not enough," I said. "Prevention doesn't work without understanding. If we don't know what we're dealing with, how can we be prepared?"

"And you're asking me?" Annie smirked, rolling her eyes at me. "I don't have a General's insignia on my jacket, do I? Besides, I get their reasoning. Their priority is to ensure everyone's safety."

She continued to talk, defending her point of view, the general's point of view, whoever. But I was no longer really processing anything she was saying.

Even though I gave her the occasional nod, my mind was already working at a thousand miles per hour, trying to see this Puppet Master situation from all angles.

There were so many tests I could conduct, if given the chance.

Would any of my equipment work on the vines? What if I could get closer in, find the main plant? It was a plant, right?

If there was any intelligence, any real pattern, the vines were probably just an extension of this Puppet Master. And if that was the case, there had to be a nerve center of sorts. If I were to conduct any tests, I would have to find out its location.

Of course, that was impossible. My shoulders sank.

I wasn't invited to any of the government groups tackling the situation, and the government wasn't exactly sharing what they knew with the civilians. All I had were hypothesis and conjectures. And, if it weren't for Annie, I wouldn't even have that.

"Why the hell is this being kept a secret?" I said out loud, voicing my own thoughts. Annie just stopped whatever it was she was saying, her eyes wide with surprise, and then a frown took over her face.

"You weren't listening to me, were you?" She asked, and all I could do was shrug sheepishly.

"Sorry," I apologized, but I couldn't stop myself from hitting her with a follow-question. "But, seriously, why doesn't the government share what they know? Maybe not to the civilians, but there a lot of scientists in the city that could help."

"The timing just isn't that great," Annie sighed. "With all the anti-alien sentiment going around, the General probably feels it's better not to stir the pot. I mean, how easy would it be for the anti-alien groups to say this Puppet Master is the alien's fault?"

"True," I agreed.

"One step at a time, I guess," she shrugged. "The General has already set up the public enquiry office, so that's something."

"The enquiry office…" I repeated, remembering something I had seen on the holonews a few days ago. "The project spearheaded by that woman, what was here name, Stacy something?"

"Stasia. Stasia Cole. She used to work here, can you believe it? She proposed it as a way to bridge the communication gap between the aliens and the humans. I'm not sure if it'll work, though. People are stubborn, and the anti-alien propaganda is strong."

"People will see the light," I said, choosing to believe most people would see through the propaganda.

"Well, some people are actually going to the office," she shrugged, "although I guess most of them just go there to complain."

"Maybe someone should go there to ask questions

instead of complaints," I mused, an idea already brewing inside my head.

Annie just pursed her lips, her forehead creasing with concern.

"Don't do anything stupid, Daphne."

"Me?" I laughed. "Never!"

Takar

I WOKE UP IN DARKNESS, which wasn't terribly unusual. I almost always woke up well before the sun painted the sky. Today, however, was darker than others. It was a combination of the heavy clouds bringing down the non-stop, yet gentle rain since yesterday, and my mood. Today, I was to play "Complaint Officer." A light growl escaped my lips.

There was only one light on in the apartment, the one for the cleansing room, and it was something small that plugged into the electrical socket.

No matter how old we grew, Rokul still needed at least that light on. He could sleep in utter darkness, but when it was time to use the cleansing room, if he didn't have some sort of light on, he'd curse and fumble around in the dark, occasionally missing the mark and making a mess.

My brother was, by far, the most unusual person I had ever met. Even now, with Tella part of his life—and part of his bed—he was still the same person he had been while we were growing up.

I quietly tip-toed passed their room on my way to the cleansing room. Once inside, I closed the door, turned on the light, and went about my morning routine.

As I washed myself in the shower, I thought about the Enquiry Office that General Rouhr had created in order to appease the whiney humans. Granted, not all of them were annoying cry-babies, but why we had to listen to their complaints and give them either answers or advice on how to deal with those complaints…what was the point? All the humans needed to do was trust that we were doing what was right.

They had never faced the Xathi before, they didn't know what kind of cleanup was involved after a Xathi attack. *Where did he put my toothpaste? Of course he put it there.* We were doing what was necessary, why couldn't they just accept that?

Why should they, as a collective, know as much as we did? I didn't know everything that the General did, and I didn't want to know. Back in the war, before the rift, I didn't know what the War Council did and that was fine with me. If I had a complaint, *spit, rinse, spit,* I dealt with it myself or learned to accept that there were just things I didn't like.

I cleaned up after myself, making sure the cleansing room, or bathroom, was as clean as it was before I used it.

There was light streaming out from under Rokul and Tella's room. "Morning," I said as I walked by.

"Morning," I heard Tella groan, then she yelped and started cursing at Rokul as he laughed. He must have pinched her, again. He had started doing that fairly often lately and it was going to get him in trouble.

I made myself a simple breakfast of eggs, bacon, and something Tella called oatmeal. It tasted better than the breakfast gruel I used to eat on the ship, so I was content. As the couple came to join me in the kitchen, I was already finishing off my last bite.

"You're on Complaint Officer duty, right?" Rokul asked, which put me into a more sour mood. To match my mood, thunder clapped outside and the rain intensified slightly.

"Yes," I grumbled as I rose from the table to wash my plate.

"Ooh, Stuffy is grumpy today," Tella teased using the nickname for me that she had fashioned. "Come on, it's not that bad. You just have to sit down and pretend to listen to people. I do it with you two every day."

"Hey!" Rokul exclaimed in mock indignation.

While they laughed, I gathered my gear, double checked my weaponry to ensure that they were properly cleaned, loaded, and stored, then bid them good-day. The rain was still gentle, but annoyingly cold. It was a sign that the seasons were about to change. I wondered what winter on Ankau would look like, or if the planet was in a perpetual state of late spring/early summer.

I ensured my pack was closed and that my rifle was covered, then stepped out into the rain. I marched to the General's office building only to be greeted by a line of humans waiting outside…already. I stepped into the building, sloughed myself off from one of the many towels Tobias had placed by the door, and headed to the room that General Rouhr had specifically set aside for human complaints and named it with a sign, subtitled, "Complaints and Redress".

The room itself was fairly simple, and comfortable by human standards. There was a big wooden desk with an overly comfortable chair—easily my favorite chair in this city, although I would never admit it—for me to sit in, three other semi-comfortable chairs arranged in front of the desk, a couch, and in a corner, a small table with things to do for children.

I looked over the list of issues that were still unanswered from the day before, resigned myself to having to deal with people complaining about not getting their complaints dealt with, and buzzed Tobias. "Let them in," I said dejectedly.

Over the next several hours, including during my lunch break, I listened to complaints about the lack of food, how bland the simulated food was, questions about why we haven't fixed a neighborhood yet, at least two people with nothing better to do than simply throw insults at me, and a complaint about the lack of suitable technology at one of the schools.

Alright. The last one was something would be interested in doing something about.

Nothing was more important than learning. Learning leads to knowledge, which led to proper preparedness, which led to not getting caught by surprise and being capable of completing whatever task needed to be completed.

I made that one a priority and sent it off to Tu'ver, Sylor, and Iq'her. They were collectively in charge of trying to improve the technology of the city.

Finally, there was one more…a woman by the name of Daphne March. Her 'complaint' was that she was nervous about the fate of her city. *Well, if these damn humans would just trust us to know what was best and allow us to handle our responsibilities, there would be nothing to be nervous about. These recking idiots that are part of the 'anti-alien' group just needed to shut the reck up and stay out of our way. We would leave soon enough.*

If we could.

Of course, no matter what my thoughts were, the likelihood of us leaving was evaporating more and more every day. Too many of us were getting close to the humans, developing friendships and relationships with them. I was certain that Vrehx and Rouhr would stay here if we had the chance to leave.

I worried that Rokul would stay, as well.

I looked up as this Daphne person entered the room. A petite brunette, she looked around every corner, curiosity lighting her eyes.

Her distraction gave me a moment to collect myself. It seemed unthinkable that anyone would be able to look as attractive as her in a war ravaged city. She had her hair tied up in what was commonly referred to as a top-knot, but stray strands fell to soften the look. My hand itched to push the silky strands back behind her ear.

I fought the feeling, realizing the eager smile on her face seemed very out of place for someone that was 'nervous.'

"How can I help you, Miss March?" I asked in my most professional voice, not really caring what her response was going to be as I stared her body up and down. She was voluptuous and curvy and in my mind one of the prettiest humans I had ever laid eyes upon.

She fairly bounced across the room and into one of

the chairs across from me. She seemed to be far too happy to be here.

"Hi. I was wondering if you could tell me about the Puppet Master."

My head snapped up from my perusal of my paperwork. She sat there, smiling at me.

"I'm sorry," I said trying to focus. "I was under the impression that you were here to discuss your nervousness about the city."

"Yeah, I know," she replied, her voice far too energetic and peppy. "I lied. I'm really here to get more information about whatever that thing is that's responsible for the plants."

This was entirely too disconcerting. She wasn't afraid. She was interested.

About something she shouldn't know anything about.

I needed to know what she knew already, so I asked her.

That was possibly a mistake.

She talked, and talked, and talked. Sometimes her sentences were about what she knew, but most of the time it was about what her thoughts were of it and what she thought those thoughts meant. It was like listening to Axtin go on and on about one of his battles.

As of Axtin's latest telling of how he saved Leena from the Xathi ship, he destroyed nearly a hundred

Xathi with his bare hands and that infernal hammer of his.

Daphne finally stopped talking. "So?" She asked, proving me a liar on the 'stopped talking' part. "What can you tell me?"

"I can tell you that we're doing the best we can to contain the situation and determine a proper course of action," I answered.

"But what course of action are you taking? Do you know if the Puppet Master is intelligent? Can it talk? Have you tried communicating with it? What if we can't fix things?" She threw out so many questions, I lost track of what she was saying.

"Why did you lie about your concerns?" I asked as a way of stopping her.

She shrugged and smiled at me. "I didn't think you'd tell me anything if I just asked outright."

"I see. Well, in regards to the Puppet Master, it is a creature that we are currently studying and determining the best course of action in how to deal with it," I explained. "We are looking into new ways to save the vegetation that we all use." I held up my hand to stop from talking any more. "I will pass on your concerns to the city leaders in an attempt to find more information. Thank you for expressing your concerns and I hope your day improves."

"But, what about…"

"Ma'am, I must apologize but I have other people that I need to speak with. It's time to go," I said as I stood up and made my way to the door. I held it open for her as she left. She opened her mouth to say something, but I closed the door and returned to the desk.

I wondered who she had talked to before me.

And when I'd get the chance to talk to her again.

GET TAKAR NOW!

https://elinwynbooks.com/conquered-world-alien-romance/

And don't forget the Facebook group, where I post sneak peeks of chapters and covers!

https://www.facebook.com/groups/ElinWyn/

Given: Star Breed Book One

When a renegade thief and a genetically enhanced mercenary collide, space gets a whole lot hotter!

Thief Kara Shimsi has learned three lessons well - keep her head down, her fingers light, and her tithes to the syndicate paid on time.

But now a failed heist has earned her a death sentence - a one-way ticket to the toxic Waste outside the dome. Her only chance is a deal with the syndicate's most ruthless enforcer, a wolfish mountain of genetically-modified muscle named Davien.

The thought makes her body tingle with dread-or is it heat?

Mercenary Davien has one focus: do whatever is necessary to get the credits to get off this backwater mining colony and back into space. The last thing he wants is a smart-mouthed thief - even if she does have the clue he needs to hunt down whoever attacked the floating lab he and his created brothers called home.

Caring is a liability. Desire is a commodity. And love could get you killed.

https://elinwynbooks.com/star-breed/

ABOUT THE AUTHOR

I love old movies – *To Catch a Thief*, *Notorious*, *All About Eve* — and anything with Katherine Hepburn in it. Clever, elegant people doing clever, elegant things.

I'm a hopeless romantic.

And I love science fiction and the promise of space.

So it makes perfect sense to me to try to merge all of those loves into a new science fiction world, where dashing heroes and lovely ladies have adventures, get into trouble, and find their true love in the stars!

www.ingramcontent.com/pod-product-compliance
Lightning Source LLC
Chambersburg PA
CBHW071913210626
46818CB00015BA/2899